REVELATION

D0013511

REVELATION

A NOVEL BY

KATE BRIAN

SIMON PULSE

New York   London   Toronto   Sydney

SIMON PULSE
An imprint of Simon & Schuster Children's Publishing Division
1230 Avenue of the Americas, New York, NY 10020

Produced by Alloy Entertainment
151 West 26th Street, New York, NY 10001

Typography by Andrea C. Uva
The text of this book was set in Filosofia.

Manufactured in the United States of America
First Simon Pulse edition September 2008

2 4 6 8 10 9 7 5 3 1

Library of Congress Control Number 2008921948

ISBN-13: 978-1-4169-5883-3
ISBN-10: 1-4169-5883-5

For B. V., who decided his due date should be the same day
as the due date for this novel

REVELATION

NOT AGAIN

The dread was like smoldering black embers right in the pit of my stomach. I knew the sensation well. Used to feel it every day after school as I approached my house in Croton, Pennsylvania, not knowing what might be going on inside. Never knowing in what condition I might find my mother. Passed out with a bottle of pills spilled on the floor? Manically cleaning the kitchen in her pajamas? Angrily waiting to scold me for something I hadn't done? Yes, I knew dread all too well. I had just never felt dread like this upon my return to Easton Academy.

It was the Sunday of Thanksgiving weekend, and, thanks to my Billings House fund money, it was the first time I'd flown back to Easton. When I had said good-bye to my parents that morning at the airport I had actually felt a pull to stay. It was so ironic. Now that my mother was better, leaving home was the hard part, and it was coming back to school that was giving me the dry heaves. But who could blame me, considering the pariah I had become at Easton?

The cab driver pulled up in front of Bradwell, the freshman and sophomore girls' dorm. I paid him and struggled out of the car with my backpack, duffel bag, and laptop. It was frigid outside, and a cold wind whipped through the trees along the drive. I had expected the campus to feel more alive since all the students were supposed to be returning from break. But though there were a few lit windows dotting the brick facades of the three girls' dorms on the circle, there wasn't a soul in sight. I took a deep breath and started along the cobblestone walk between Bradwell and Pemberly, my heart pounding with each heavy step as I drew closer to the quad.

I didn't want to go back to Billings House. I so wasn't ready.

When I reached the far side of Bradwell, I paused and gazed across the quad at Billings, the tallest dorm on campus. Instantly, the embers of dread burned brighter. It had been just over a week since the Billings fund-raiser in New York City—the event that should have been the most amazing night of my life. Instead it had been the most humiliating. It had been the night when a video of me and Dash McCafferty getting all gropey at the Legacy had been sent out to every cell phone and BlackBerry at school. Everyone had seen me and Dash—my best friend Noelle Lange's boyfriend—kissing. Touching. Taking off each other's clothes. Everyone knew what I had done. And no one had talked to me since.

Except Sabine DuLac, my roommate in Billings.

Where Noelle had all but banned me from the Billings table in the dining hall, where Portia Ahronian had organized a Billings shopping trip and excluded me, and where even Kiki Rosen had switched seats in the library so she wouldn't have to acknowledge me—Sabine had remained loyal. At least I had one true friend left. One person who had been willing to listen to my explanation. Although, she had always hated Noelle. She probably would have taken my side if I'd shot the girl dead. But maybe now that a few days had passed, some of the others would come around as well. Maybe I could even get Noelle to listen to me.

It was a stretch, I knew. But I was going to have to try.

Halfway across the snow-covered quad, lit only by the quaint, ground-level lamps lining the pathways, I stopped and took a deep breath to steel myself. I was going to march into Billings and I was going to make Noelle listen to me. I didn't care if I had to scream the whole apology to her through her closed dorm-room door. She was going to hear my side.

My life at Easton depended on it.

A bitter gust of wind whipped my dark hair back from my face and got me moving again. Knees quaking—not from nerves, I told myself, but from the cold and the weight of my bags—I turned up the walk to Billings. That was when I saw a dark figure move toward me. I froze.

"Reed. Good. I'm glad I caught you."

It was Detective Hauer. The King of Bad News. Just what I needed.

"Detective," I said. He was all bundled up in a dark wool coat that seemed one size too small for his stocky frame, a tweed hat pulled low over his brow, hiding his dark, usually unkempt hair. His wide nose was red from the cold, and there were visible bags under his brown eyes. The way he looked at me—like a doctor probably looks at a patient right before he diagnoses inoperable cancer—made me want to run inside, even though I dreaded facing my friends.

"What?" I said finally.

"I just wanted to give you the heads up," he said, holding his hat as another gust of wind nearly knocked me off my feet. "Since you've been so cooperative during this . . . uh . . . tragedy." Hauer hesitated, his eyes darting away from my face.

What was with this guy? He was an adult and a police officer. He was not supposed to feel nervous when talking to me.

"We've found new evidence," he said. "Your friend Cheyenne Martin . . . She was definitely murdered."

His words sucked all the air from my lungs and I clutched the handle on my duffel bag, as if that would keep me from fainting dead away. This wasn't possible. Not again. Not another murder. Cheyenne had OD'd. We had all been there to find her. We had all read her suicide note. She had even sent me an e-mail saying I was the reason she killed herself—an e-mail that had haunted me for months now. Plus, no one had heard a struggle. There'd been no blood, no bruises, nothing broken in her room. How could this be possible?

"What?" I heard myself say as the wind whistled overhead. "You can't be serious."

A couple of weeks back Detective Hauer had told me the case was going to be reopened at Cheyenne's parents' request, but at the time even he still thought it was a clear-cut suicide.

"Unfortunately, I am," he said, shoving his hands in his pockets.

"I don't understand," I said, my mind racing. "What new evidence?

How can there be new evidence *now*? She died months ago. She was cremated. Her room's not even a crime scene—Noelle's been living there for weeks. What could you have possibly found?"

The detective cleared his throat. "I'm afraid that information is classified."

"Classified? Is this a government conspiracy now?" I blurted, frustrated.

He leveled me with an admonishing glare. "It's not for public consumption," he clarified sternly. "But you should know we're going to be reinterviewing everyone of interest," he added, standing up straight. He sounded surer of himself now, and fixed me with a steady-eyed gaze. "If there's anything else you want to tell me, now is the time."

"Anything else?" I stood there, unable to think. Unable to breathe. Unable to move. Cheyenne had been murdered. I was going to have to tell the rest of Billings about this. Yeah, right. If they'd even stay in the same room with me for five seconds.

"Yes. Anything at all," he said.

Behind Hauer, I saw a group of girls walking in a huddle toward Pemberly. One of them noticed us and lifted her chin, and another girl turned.

Ivy Slade.

Her coal-black eyes fixed on me, and a cold bolt of ice slammed into my heart. She looked at Hauer and a sly smile lit her pointy face. Clearly she was already calculating how quickly she could spread the news that the cops were talking to me, but I didn't care. All I could think about was her story. Her hatred of Billings. Her promise that she would bring us all down.

After the Billings fund-raiser she had told me everything. How the Billings Girls had forced her and the other Billings hopefuls to break into her grandmother's house her sophomore year to steal a family heirloom. How they had tripped the alarm, which had caused her grandmother to have a stroke that ultimately killed her. How Noelle, Ariana, Cheyenne, and the other Billings Girls had left Ivy there to cope with the tragedy herself.

If Cheyenne had definitely been murdered, then Ivy was, in my opinion, suspect number one. The girl had motive seeping out her pores. She had practically told me straight out that she was going to get revenge on Noelle as well as destroy Billings. Plus, I already knew she was capable of very bad things. Ever since Cheyenne had died, someone had been stalking me. Leaving artifacts from Cheyenne's life tucked around my room for me to find. Taking that video of me and Dash and sending it to the entire student body. It was Ivy. I was sure of it. My certainty, of course, had nothing to do with the fact that she'd stolen the love of my life, Josh Hollis.

"Ivy Slade," I said under my breath, as the girls turned and continued on their merry way.

"What was that?" Detective Hauer asked, curving his shoulders against the wind.

"Ivy Slade," I said more loudly.

The detective sighed and blew on his chapped hands. "Reed, we already talked to her," he said finally. "She's not our girl."

"Talk to her again," I told him through my teeth.

"Reed, we can't waste our time on—"

"I'm telling you, Detective, it's not a waste of time," I said, my blood racing now. "That girl is capable of murder. I know she is. And she hated Cheyenne. Last week she even threatened Noelle."

This caught his attention. "Threatened to kill her?"

"Well, no. Not in those words, but—"

Suddenly, the detective looked extremely tired. "Look, unless you have some real evidence against the girl, there's nothing I can do."

His tone was condescending and impatient. Like I was just some stupid kid spreading rumors. I retightened my fingers around the strap of my duffel bag.

"You haven't gotten the whole story," I said, trying to keep my voice even. "Believe me."

Hauer blew out a sigh and looked up at the starless night. "How about we start with your story?" he suggested. "I know we already talked about the . . . uh, letter, you received from Ms. Martin's e-mail account the night she died and your contentious friendship with her. But I need your official statement. Where you were at the time of Ms. Martin's death . . . who you were with. . . ."

I felt fire burning from my eyes. He needed *my* statement when a psycho like Ivy was strolling around campus free and clear?

"You want my statement? Fine. Here it is," I said, drawing myself up straight. "At the time of the murder I was asleep in my bed while my roommate was asleep in hers. I woke up to the sound of screaming and ran down the hall to find the president of my dorm dead on the floor of her room. That's all I know. Now why don't you go interview someone with, oh, I don't know, a motive?"

Hauer gave me an exasperated look, but I no longer cared to humor him. I turned around and stormed up to Billings, suddenly feeling more confident than ever that I could take on Noelle and the rest of my friends. Had to love a good adrenaline rush.

At least Detective Hauer was good for something.

OUT

I was all confident bravado until I walked into the Billings foyer and got that eerie, sickening feeling that I had just caused an abrupt silence. Slowly, I turned toward the parlor. From my vantage point I could see a few of my Billings sisters crowded onto the gold brocade love seat. Astrid Chou glanced over at me and quickly slouched down, drawing her hand up to her cheek as if to hide her face.

Dead silence. Aside from the cozy crackling of the fire, there was nothing. My mouth was dryer than a sandbox.

Move, Reed. Move.

I placed my bags on the floor and walked toward the parlor, stripping off my coat, scarf, and gloves as I went, since my inner thermometer was now registering about four thousand degrees. With each inch I could see a bit more of the room, and by the time I reached the door, my suspicions were confirmed.

Every last Billings Girl was gathered around the parlor. Portia

Ahronian, Shelby Wordsworth, London Simmons, and Vienna Clark were on the couch, all avoiding my gaze. Kiki Thorpe, Missy Thurber, and Lorna Gross were crowded onto the love seat next to Astrid. Tiffany Goulbourne and Rose Sakowitz sat in the straight-backed chairs in front of the flat-screen TV. Even Constance Talbot and Sabine DuLac were there, sitting on the floor with their legs curled under the coffee table. And at the head of the room, perched in the wingback chair near the fireplace, was Noelle Lange. Her thick dark hair was pulled back in a bun and she wore a black turtleneck sweater and a black and gray plaid skirt. Huge diamonds sparkled in her ears. Her full lips twisted into a semblance of a smile as she looked me in the eye—the only person able to do so.

"What's going on?" I said tentatively. The sound of my voice made a few of the girls squirm. Cleary this was a scheduled meeting. Clearly they had all known to get back to campus early for this. And clearly, Noelle was at the heart of it.

I stared at Sabine, who stared down at her knee-high leather booths. Why hadn't she warned me about this?

"Perfect timing, Reed," Noelle said, leaning back. Her elbows casually perched on the chair's armrests as she coolly looked me over. She lifted both hands, palms up, and her dark eyes sparkled merrily. "We just voted you out."

The earth tilted beneath my feet. She couldn't have said what I thought I'd heard. Not so cavalierly. She couldn't. But no one was laughing like it was a joke. No one even moved. I gripped the back of the love seat, my sweaty fingers pulling on Lorna's wavy brown hair.

"Ow!" Lorna protested loudly, sitting forward to free herself.

"What do you mean, you voted me out?" I breathed. Suddenly everything in the room was distorted. The faces, the furniture, the flames leaping in the fireplace. It wasn't real. This couldn't be real.

"You have an hour to pack your things," Noelle said, standing and smoothing her skirt. "There's a single waiting for you in Pemberly."

My mind reeled, making me feel dizzy, unsteady. Grappling to stay focused, I looked around at my so-called friends. At the people with whom I had shared so much. At the girls who had voted me president just two months ago. *Unanimously* voted me president. We studied together, shopped together, gossiped together, got over hangovers together, bitched about parents and boyfriends and teachers together. They were my friends. The first real girlfriends I had ever had. The first real family I'd ever had. They couldn't do this to me. They wouldn't.

"No. You guys. You can't just—"

"Sure we can," Noelle said with a smirk, stepping over outstretched legs and designer shoes to stand before me. "The residents of Billings decide who lives in Billings, remember? And we decided we don't want a backstabbing bitch living here."

My grip on the love seat tightened. I couldn't breathe. I stared into Noelle's cool brown eyes, searching for the punch line. Waiting for her to laugh and tell me she was just messing with me like she had so many times in the past. We were friends. Practically sisters. And yeah, I had messed up, but didn't a person even get a chance to beg for forgiveness before . . . this?

"No," I said finally. "No. I don't believe you."

I tore my eyes from Noelle and looked around again. I looked at Tiffany, who had always been so levelheaded and good-natured. Who had always been a voice of reason. She simply turned her face to the side, giving me a view of her perfect cheekbone and smooth cocoa skin. I glanced at Rose—sweet, don't-rock-the-boat Rose—but her eyes were trained on her lap, her red curls hiding her face. Portia rolled her big green eyes when I looked her way, and the Twin Cities studied their perfectly manicured nails. Only Constance and Sabine looked at me, silently begging for forgiveness.

The reality washed over me. It was true. They had all turned on me. They had voted to kick me out of the dorm I had just saved for them—the dorm I had raised five million dollars for in order to keep Headmaster Cromwell from shutting us down. The dorm I had lived in all last year—longer than many of them. This was my home. And they were taking it away from me.

"Who voted me out?" I asked, my voice clear as a bell.

I was angry and desperate and grasping at straws, but I needed to know. I needed to know exactly who had turned on me. And I couldn't just surrender and slink out of there with my tail between my legs. I refused.

Noelle scoffed at my question. Everyone else exchanged troubled glances. Disbelieving glances. Like asking them to tell me which of them were traitors was so very gauche. As if I cared about gauche right then.

"Who voted me out?" I said again. "I want to know."

Missy Thurber's hand was the first to go up. Shocker. Girl and her Chunnel-size nostrils had always hated my guts. But then, ever so slowly, more hands started to rise. Lorna's, Shelby's, Portia's. Even Kiki, Rose, Tiffany, and the Twin Cities had voted against me. People who a week ago I would have counted among my good friends. Only three sets of hands stayed firmly planted in their owners' laps.

Sabine, Constance, and Astrid had taken my side. That was it. That was all I had. Three real friends.

The burning dread in my gut slowly hardened into heavy, cold, sorrow.

"Sorry, Glass-Licker," Noelle said with a tilt of her head. "Looks like you're going back to where you've always belonged."

Back to where I always belonged? Was she kidding? She was the one who had always told me that I belonged *here*. She was the one who had insisted that Billings House needed me. How could she possibly look me in the eye and say that?

Noelle started by me, brushing my shoulder with hers. Indignant anger flared beneath my shock, and I heard myself speak.

"I don't think so."

Everyone in the room sucked in a breath. I wasn't even sure that I still wanted to live there, knowing they had all turned against me. But I wasn't about to give Noelle the satisfaction of seeing me go down without a fight. Not a chance.

"Excuse me?" Noelle said incredulously, swinging around to face me.

"That whole 'Billings decides who lives in Billings' rule doesn't apply anymore, remember?" I said, summoning all my courage to square off with her. "Not since Headmaster Cromwell overruled it at the beginning of the year. I'm not going anywhere."

Noelle's eyes cut through me like tiny little knives. She didn't even have to speak for me to know she'd already found a way around this.

"You'd like to think that, wouldn't you?" she said, looking down her nose at me. "But when I single-handedly delivered the Crom a check for more than five million dollars to use as he pleases, he pretty much intimated that I can do whatever I want around here."

Single-handedly? As if I hadn't worked my ass off on that fundraiser.

"And what I want is you out," she finished, her lips curving into a smirk. "Don't make it worse by getting all pathetic and whiny about it."

My face burned like I'd been in the sun for four days straight. She was loving every minute of this. Loved humiliating me in front of everyone. Loved seeing me suffer. I hated her so much in that moment, I wanted to tear her hair out. And yet, I still wanted her to change her mind. Still wanted her to put her arm around me and tell me everything was going to be fine. I still wanted her approval. The fact that I had potentially lost it forever might have been the most devastating realization of all.

"Come on, ladies," Noelle said to the room. "I brought back some gifties from the city."

Just like that, everyone was out of their seats, happily bustling for the door. They all slipped around me as if I were a muddy puddle they were trying to avoid. I just stood there. I couldn't have moved if I wanted to. And after what they had done to me, I wasn't about to get out of their way. It was a small defiance, but it was all I had.

"Noelle, please don't do this," I said under my breath, stepping up to her once the room was all but empty. I didn't want to beg. I didn't want to explain myself while my blood was still hot with anger. But I sensed this could be my last chance. "I was drunk. I thought you guys were broken up. I am so, *so* sorry."

For a split second I saw the depth of the hurt Noelle was feeling reflected in her eyes and it stopped my heart. I had destroyed her. My best friend. The person who had been there for me through some of the worst moments of my life. I had hurt her beyond all repair. All of this, this huge scene, was just her way of protecting herself. Her way of saving face. My guilt compounded exponentially. I deserved her punishment. I did. But did it have to be this?

Suddenly, she turned her head to the side and blinked. When she looked at me again, the imperious stare was back.

"It doesn't matter what you thought," she said, crossing her arms over her chest. "Dash was and is mine. And even if we had been broken up, you don't go there. Not with a friend's ex."

I blinked and Noelle smirked.

"Yes, Reed. I know you're dying for an update, so here it is. Dash and I are still together and we're always going to be together," she said. "One moment of weakness on his part is not going to change that. Especially when you so clearly threw yourself at him."

That was beyond untrue. *Dash* had been the one to invite me to one of the secluded tents on the roof at the Legacy. *Dash* had been the one to initiate things once I got there. But clearly either he or Noelle had decided to rewrite history so they could move on with their life together. Somehow, all the blame was being laid squarely on my shoulders.

"But don't worry. Fair is fair," she told me, lifting her chin. "You're not the only one being punished. He will be groveling for a long, *long* time."

"Noelle, I'm sorry for what happened," I said, wiping my sweaty hands on my jeans. "You're right. I stepped over the line. And I'll do anything to make it up to you. But Noelle, come on. This is between you and me. You didn't have to drag the whole dorm into it."

A smile slowly twisted its way across Noelle's face. "I didn't. The vote wasn't even my idea."

I blinked, stunned. "What?"

"Have you forgotten everything, Reed? This is what Billings is all about. We take care of each other," she said lightly. "Even when it means deciding between two sisters and turning our backs on the one in the wrong."

My heart felt sick. Sick and black and sour. How many times had she told me this in the past? That she would always take care of me, always watch out for me, because that was what Billings was all about.

But now I no longer had a right to that privilege. Now she was taking that all away.

"One hour," Noelle said, tapping her gold watch once. Her tone was so final it weakened my knees. "The clock's ticking."

Then she turned her back on me and was gone.

PUSH BACK

Packing. I was packing up my room. I was no longer welcome in Billings, the only place I had ever really wanted to live. As I shakily removed my clothes from the dresser and placed them in my larger suitcase, I realized my heart had never felt this heavy. It might as well have been made out of lead.

"We tried to talk them out of it, but they wouldn't hear of it," Astrid said in her thick British accent. She was slowly, reluctantly, folding up my bedding and stashing it in a large green garbage bag someone had fished out of a supply closet. This was how low I had sunk. Garbage bags as luggage. "It's a bunch of bollocks if you ask me. Everyone trips up now and again, right? We're only human."

"I think a lot of the girls wanted to vote for you to stay, but everyone's afraid of Noelle," Constance added. Hovering by the closet, she tugged on a lock of her red hair over and over and over again, eyeing me nervously like I might be on the verge of a breakdown. At least

Constance was speaking to me again. After the fund-raiser she hadn't even been able to look at me, unable to believe I had backstabbed Noelle. Apparently the thought of me getting booted for it, however, had seemed unfair punishment to her. Neither she nor Sabine had done anything to speed along the process of moving me out. Clearly they were still having as hard a time with this as I was.

"Is there anything we can do?" Sabine asked, sitting on the end of her bed, her green eyes probing mine.

Anything they could do. Like what? Plead my case to Noelle for me? Tie her down and make her listen? Build me a time machine so I could go back to the Legacy and *not* hook up with Dash?

"Help me pack?" I suggested with a sad smile.

Sabine and Constance looked at each other and seemed to come to a grim agreement. Constance turned toward the closet and Sabine got up to help her take the sweaters off the top shelf.

"God, I hate Noelle," Sabine said. "Someone should really give her a nice kick in the—"

At that moment the door to our room swung open and Noelle strode in. Sabine's mouth snapped shut and we all froze. Had she heard what Sabine had been saying? If so, she showed no sign. Her attention was focused on me.

"I want all your Billings things back," she said, her arms crossed over her chest.

I blinked. "Billings things? What Billings things?"

Noelle rolled her eyes. "The Chloé bag, to start. And any other gifts the alumni stashed inside of it. What did they give you? Cash? A credit card? Whatever it is, I'll take it now." She held out a hand and flicked her fingers, like I was just going to drop it all in her palm.

This was a test. I could feel it. Noelle was trying to see just how far she could push me. I knew from experience that I had to push right back.

"No," I said, lifting my chin defiantly.

"Excuse me?" Noelle replied, her eyes narrowing.

"No. I'm not giving you the bag or anything else," I told her. I couldn't give in to her. Couldn't show weakness. Not if I ever hoped to win back her respect. "Those gifts were given to me. They're mine."

"They were gifts given to you when you were president of Billings," Noelle said, taking a menacing step toward me. "You no longer live here. You have no right to—"

"Sorry, but I think I have every right to keep the things that were given to me as gifts," I said, trying to be blithe even as my heart pounded in my temples. "They didn't come with a disclaimer."

To punctuate my point, I picked up the gorgeous leather Chloé bag and dumped it into Astrid's garbage bag along with my bedding. Noelle glared at me for a long moment, then sighed, like I was just so juvenile.

"Fine. But I will be taking back the disc," she said. "That cannot remain in the possession of a nonresident."

My face prickled with heat. No one else in the room knew about the disc.

"Disc? What disc?" Sabine asked, her green eyes suddenly curious.

"Noelle," I said through my teeth. "I haven't told anyone about the—"

"It's this disc that was given to Reed by the alums," Noelle said loudly, addressing Sabine. "It's chock-full of inside info on all of us—on anyone who has ever lived in Billings. She's had it all semester, Sabine. I'm surprised she didn't share it with you, of all people."

Bitch. Total bitch. It wasn't enough she was throwing me out. Now she was trying to drive a wedge between me and Sabine.

"Inside info?" Astrid asked tentatively. "What kind of inside info?"

"Like stuff about our families and stuff?" Constance said, wide-eyed.

"Like stuff about our past?" Sabine added.

The tension in the room was palpable. All three of them were completely freaked by the idea that I might know their secrets. Noelle, meanwhile, smiled like the Cheshire cat.

"I haven't read any of your files," I said, looking around at Sabine, Constance, and Astrid. "I wouldn't do that." Then I paused and glanced at Noelle. "To you guys, at least," I added in a leading way.

I had never looked at Noelle's file, either, but why not let her think I had? She deserved a touch of paranoia considering what she was putting me through. But of course her smile didn't falter.

"The disc, Reed," she said. "You know you have no right to it now."

There was no point in arguing this. I could tell she wasn't about to give up. And now more than anything I just wanted to get her out of my room. I turned around and grabbed my portable CD case, then flipped to the John Mayer CD in the back. From behind it, I extracted the Billings disc, which I'd placed there after looking at my own file last month. As I turned around, Sabine, Constance, and Astrid all stared at the disc as if it were a nuclear bomb. I looked down at it. This tiny thing held so much power. Did I really want to give it to Noelle right in front of them? Was I really going to sell out the only people who had been faithful to me in this whole mess?

Answer? No.

I placed the disc along the edge of my desk and lifted my fist.

Noelle stepped forward. "What are you—"

But she was too late. I brought my hand down on the side that was hanging over the edge of the desk. The thing split right in half with a satisfying crack.

"Huh. I can't believe that worked," I said. I turned and Frisbeed the two halves at Noelle's feet. "There you go. There's your precious disc."

Everyone just stared down at the broken pieces.

"That's fine," Noelle said finally. "They'll send me a new one." She checked her watch. "Reed, you have thirty-three minutes."

She slammed the door on her way out, and everyone let out a breath. Astrid dropped to the ground to pick up the pieces of the disc.

"How bad was it, really?" she asked me, her dark eyes nervous as she held up the remnants.

"I really only looked at mine, but it was bad," I told her. "It listed my parents' income, how much I made last summer, all my exes. . . . There was even stuff on my brother on there."

"Scary," Astrid said, launching the pieces into Sabine's plastic garbage can.

"Do you really think she can just get another one?" Sabine asked.

"Probably," I said with a shrug. "But you guys are all pretty normal," I joked. "You have nothing to worry about, right?"

"Right," they all chorused, looking at one another in a snagged way.

Then we all cracked up laughing. I couldn't imagine that the secrets in their files were anything all that awful. Maybe to them they were, but considering some of the secrets people like Ariana and Cheyenne had kept, how bad could they be?

"Come on. You heard her," I said flatly. "We only have thirty-three minutes."

"I can't believe this is really happening," Sabine said, getting back to work. She shook her long black hair back from her shoulders and her ever-present shell earrings clicked and swung. "Maybe I can put in for a transfer!" she said excitedly. "We can room together in Pemberly."

I was touched at the offer. Clearly Sabine cared more about me than Billings, which was unprecedented. But I couldn't do that to her.

"You heard what Noelle said. It's a single," I told her. "There's no way we'd ever fit. But thanks for the offer."

Sabine's face fell. "Well, then, we should just talk to everyone. Get them to vote again . . ."

"No. I don't want to be all 'pathetic and whiny about it,'" I said, quoting Noelle.

"You're right," Astrid said, shoving a throw pillow into the now bulging garbage bag. "Chin up. Screw her. That's the only way to deal with this."

"Maybe if you just go and live in Pemberly for a while she'll cool down," Constance suggested, chewing on her bottom lip. "Maybe . . . I don't know . . . maybe they'll all come around."

Pemberly. The very thought of the old, gray dorm with its tiny little windows, paint-chipped door, and ancient, abused furniture made my skin crawl. I wasn't meant for Pemberly. I was meant for Billings.

But I couldn't argue with Constance's logic. I might be better off trying to fix this thing from afar.

"This is so unfair," Sabine said. "You *are* Billings."

The words hung in the air like a funeral dirge. They all looked at me mournfully and I felt as if my heart was breaking. From my angle I could still see the two halves of the broken disc shining in the garbage can.

"Not anymore," I said.

The Pemberly single was one of the most depressing things I'd ever seen. The old wood floors were scratched and gouged, and a crusty stain seeped out from beneath the single bed. All the old, dingy furniture was shoved up against the walls—bed to my left, desk straight across, dresser to my right—leaving just enough space in the center of the room to walk through. Above the bed was one tall, skinny window with peeling paint all around the pane, and the whole thing looked like it might fall off if I tried to open it. I turned to check out the closet right next to the door. It was one-tenth the size of the one in Billings and closed over by a folding accordion door in faux wood.

Compared to my room in Billings, this was a prison cell—a really, really cold prison cell. Maybe the Crom should use some of that five mil to renovate Pemberly. These girls' parents were paying ridiculous amounts of money for them to live like inmates.

I shoved open the closet's accordion door, which instantly came off its top runner, and threw my bags inside on the floor. A dust bunny skittered across the room and I felt tears well up in my eyes. How had this happened? I had made one mistake. One big mistake, but still. That meant my whole life was over?

Okay. No crying. No crying allowed. I will not let Noelle get the better of me.

I sat down on the bed, which creaked loudly beneath my weight, and pulled my coat closer to me, wondering if the heater was working at all or if I'd have to complain to maintenance tomorrow. Through the open door I could hear laughter and music and voices from down the hall. Unfamiliar sounds. Unfamiliar people. And suddenly I was overcome with grief.

I missed my room. I missed the space and the cleanliness and the private, connected bathroom. I missed my view and my closet and the frosted lights in the ceiling and the warmth. And I missed Sabine. I missed everyone, actually. Even though they had turned on me—maybe *because* they had turned on me—I missed them so much it hurt. Couldn't they have at least given me a chance to explain? Couldn't they have given me a chance to win them back?

I pulled my knees up under my chin and was about to give in to tears when I stopped myself and stood up.

"No. I am not going to cry," I said under my breath, splaying my fingers out at my sides. "No crying allowed."

Instead, I turned and snatched up the pink sheet of paper that was propped up on something in the center of the desk. The words PEMBERLY HALL RULES AND REGULATIONS were printed at the top above a list of ten items. Rules and regulations. Yes. I could distract myself with this for about ten seconds. I was just about to start reading when I noticed the items that had been propping up the page. Both my hand and the paper fell.

A small white place card with my name handwritten in pink calligraphy sat in the center of the desk. It was my place card from Cheyenne's last official meeting as president of Billings. And in front of that was a tiny velvet bag with pills spilling out of it. White pills with a blue dot design. The pills that Cheyenne had OD'd on. No—the pills that someone had used to kill her.

I staggered back a few steps and slammed into the bit of wall between the closet and the doorway. Pain radiated up my spine, but I barely felt it. My heart was going ballistic, pounding in my ears. Who had done this? And what did it mean? Did it mean I was next? Cheyenne had died the night she was kicked out of Easton. I had just been kicked out of Billings. Had the person who had killed Cheyenne left these here for me as a warning? Did this mean I was going to die? Tonight?

I wildly checked the room as if someone was going to pop out of nowhere horror-movie style, but there was nowhere for anyone to hide. Still, my mind reeled as I clutched the pink paper in my sweaty palm. No one had known I was moving into Pemberly aside from the Billings Girls. Had someone in my old dorm left these here for me? And if so, who? Why? Why was this happening? Why couldn't whoever was doing these things just leave me alone?

"Well, well. Look who's slumming it."

A cold chill raced through me. I whirled around to find Ivy Slade leaning against my open doorway, a satisfied smirk on her witchy face. Instinctively, I backed up until I was blocking her view of the place card and pills. The very sight of her on top of what I'd just found was not good. I suddenly felt light-headed and had to clutch the desk chair behind me to keep from trembling.

"I am just *so* psyched we're going to be neighbors!" Ivy said with false exuberance.

"What . . . what're you talking about?" I said, somehow finding my voice.

Ivy took a couple of steps into the room, which left about three feet between us. At least she was toothpick-thin in her skinny jeans and flowy black top, so she didn't take up much room. As I stood there paralyzed, she looked around, her raven ponytail swinging.

"All year I've been pissed off that there was an empty single next door," she said. "I asked Cromwell to let me have it, like, a dozen times, but he refused." She paused and her black-eyed gaze flicked over me. "Maybe he knew all along that you'd end up here."

Inside, I fumed at the comment, but I couldn't seem to find a comeback nestled among my paranoia and confusion and fear.

"Actually, now that I see it, I'm glad he didn't give it to me," she said, wrinkling her nose. "It looks like no one's cleaned this place in forever. And what's that smell?" She sniffed and looked me in the eye, her own as black as pitch. "It smells like something *died* in here."

I almost choked on my own tongue.

Died. Died, died, died. Her eyes continued to bore into mine. Was it her? Had she left the pills? Was Ivy Slade going to try to kill me just like she'd killed Cheyenne?

"Well, sweet dreams!" she said merrily.

Then she turned and strode out of the room, giving me one last amused look before slamming the door behind her. I couldn't move. Could hardly even breathe. About two seconds later, loud rock music shook the wall right next to my new bed. The bitch lived right next door. Right. Next. Door. The girl who had committed herself to making my life a living hell. The girl who had snagged the love of my life. The girl who might have just subtly threatened to murder me. Right. Next. Door.

Spurred by a sudden rush of fear-tinged adrenaline, I grabbed my desk chair and shoved it under the doorknob as I had seen done in so many movies. Then I backed away, wiping my sweaty palms together, wondering if there was anything else I could do to protect myself. Even if I was wrong—even if Ivy hadn't just threatened me and her comment had been a coincidental insult—there was still a killer on campus. A killer who had just left their murder weapon in my room. There was no way I was going to sleep tonight. No way in hell.

Why was this happening to me? Why couldn't I be safely tucked into my bed in Billings right now, with Sabine just a few feet away? There was safety in numbers, right? And suddenly, I was completely alone.

Finally, the unfairness of it all overcame me. The sadistic unfairness of it all. I sat down on the cold floor, my back up against the side of my bed. Ivy's loud, angry music jolted my senses and forced the tears right out of me. I pulled my knees up and buried my face between them, clinging to my legs with both arms as I sobbed. At least with the music on, Ivy couldn't hear me. At least she wouldn't know that she'd won.

WISHES

As predicted, there was no sleep that night. Earlier I had sneaked out of the room for all of one minute to flush the pills and the place card in one of the toilets in the communal bathroom (after all, if the police were going to be investigating a murder, I didn't want to be caught with the cause of death), but they still haunted me. Every noise I heard—every creak, every whistle of wind, every footfall—brought my heart to a screeching halt and my eyes to the door. And between these excruciating moments, there were too many thoughts swirling in my mind. Too many humiliating memories popping up to replay themselves and make my heart and stomach clench. Too much to regret. Too much to wish away.

I wished I had never started e-mailing with Dash at the beginning of the school year.

I wished I hadn't had all those drinks at the Legacy.

I wished I had never gone up on that roof.

I wished Josh had never found us.

I wished I had told Noelle the truth from the beginning.

I wished I had seen Ivy taking that stupid video so that I could have bitch-slapped her right then and there and nipped this whole thing in the bud.

I pulled my pillow over my face and groaned into it. At that moment Ivy's laugh, clear as day, filled my room. I tossed the pillow aside. It wasn't just that the walls in Pemberly were paper thin—which they were—but there was a vent right beneath my bed, through which I could hear almost everything Ivy and her roommate, Jillian Crane, said to each other. At least, that is, when they were being loud and I was listening. I glanced at the clock on my desk. It was after midnight. What the hell was Ivy laughing about over there?

Her laugh was followed by a giggle and some quietly murmured words. My hands curled into fists. I recognized that tone. She was talking to a guy. Flirting. And not with just any guy—with *my* guy. Josh was, right now, whispering sweet nothings to cold, evil Ivy.

Suddenly filled with ire, I flung my covers aside and sat up straight. It was still frigid in the room, so I had worn sweatpants, a turtleneck, and a sweatshirt to bed, along with some thick socks, which now protected my feet from the icy floor as I paced in a teeny, tiny circle. I had to think. I had to figure this out once and for all. Several lives might depend on it, including my own.

Okay. Deep breath. Think. What do I actually know?

First, according to the police, Cheyenne was definitely murdered. So what did this mean exactly? It meant the suicide note had been faked. It meant that *both* suicide notes had been faked. I stopped in my tracks, suddenly seeing it all with a cold clarity. The night she died, Cheyenne hadn't sent me that haunting "Ignore the note. You did this" e-mail. She hadn't blamed me for her death. Because she hadn't intended to die at all. Whoever had sent me that e-mail was the murderer. For some reason, the murderer had wanted me to feel responsible for Cheyenne's death.

Instantly, this bizarre feeling of relief overcame me. For months I had been walking around feeling guilty, thinking that Cheyenne's last thoughts before she killed herself had been of me. Thinking that she had gone to her grave cursing me. But it wasn't true. None of it was true. Cheyenne hadn't blamed me. The very thought was like a huge boulder being lifted off my shoulders.

But of course the relief was short-lived, replaced instantly by a new and intense fear. Did this mean that my stalker was also the murderer? It made sense. The murderer had sent the e-mail, then backed it up by leaving all of these things around to remind me of Cheyenne. To torture me. To make me feel even more guilty. The pills and the place card weren't the only thing the murderer had left for me. There had been the Billings black balls, Cheyenne's pink sweater, her perfume, and all those other awful things.

My stalker was definitely the killer. Had to be. It couldn't all just be some terrifying coincidence.

I dropped back down on my bed again and clutched my comforter to my chest. The killer had been in my room at Billings several times. Had been in my closet, my drawers, my overnight bag. And he or she had been in this room too. This very day. Leaving the most horrifying message yet.

Once again I heard Ivy laugh, and my blood ran cold. It had to be her. She'd had opportunity and motive. And now I was living right next door to her—and Josh was *dating* her. I shoved the covers aside, pulled my chair out from under the doorknob, and sat down at my desk. I was not going down without a fight. Hauer wanted evidence? I'd find him some evidence. This bitch was going down.

I whipped a pad and pen out of my bag and wrote Ivy's name at the top, then jotted down all the reasons I was sure she was the bad guy. Her motive (her grandmother's stroke), her behavior (trying to exclude us from the Legacy), her not-so-subtle remarks (about hating Billings and Cheyenne). My hands shook the whole time and my writing looked like that of a serial killer—different from one line to the next—but I kept on going. When I was done, I took a deep breath. If I showed this to Hauer, would it be enough?

Probably not. Everyone knew Ivy was dating Josh now. He would probably see these as the psychotic ramblings of a teenage girl who was heartbroken that her boyfriend had moved on.

Which I was, but still.

What could I do to make it look more legit? The answer hit me almost immediately. I needed more suspects. I needed to make it at least appear like I was being fair. Unbiased. I drew my knees up and sat back in my chair to think. Part of me felt it would be a waste of time, but in all honesty, there were a few other potential suspects. Reluctantly, I listed them and their potential motives beneath Ivy's entry.

First, Trey Prescott. He was an incredible guy, and I seriously doubted he was capable of hurting a fruit fly, but he had been so angry at Cheyenne at the beginning of the year. Why had they broken up over the summer? Maybe it was something worth killing over.

Then, of course, I had to consider the other girls in Billings. They always say the people closest to the victim are the prime suspects. All the classic murder motives—jealousy, passion, anger—are stronger with people you're close to. Just look at Ariana and Thomas. She had loved him. But when it came down to it, I couldn't think of many girls with real motives for killing Cheyenne. She had been a total dictator, but most of the girls in Billings kind of liked that. The only girls with any kind of motive were the three she had targeted—the three she had wanted to kick out.

Sabine, Constance, and Lorna.

Of course I disregarded Sabine and Constance right away. They were two of my best friends and were both totally guileless, sweet, and honest. And Lorna was too big of a wuss to murder anyone, let alone spend weeks stalking me. Unless she had help from Missy, her best friend. Missy was a hell of a lot stronger than Lorna, plus she hated me. What if she had helped out Lorna by offing Cheyenne, then decided to get her own jollies by stalking me? It made a twisted kind of sense. I added "Missy/Lorna???" to my list.

After much thought I also added Astrid. It pained me to do it, but the girl was kind of an enigma. No one knew why she had been kicked out of Barton School last year. She had told me she'd been caught smoking, but would that really get a person kicked out of school?

Maybe it had been for some insidious crime. Plus she had known Cheyenne forever. Maybe, like the drama Ivy and Cheyenne had at Ivy's grandmother's house, there was something in their shared past that had set Astrid off. They had definitely been at odds with each other at the beginning of the year, and I had assumed it was because Astrid refused to fall in line with Cheyenne's plans to keep Constance, Sabine, and Lorna out of Billings. But who knew? Maybe it had been something larger than that. Still, I put two extra question marks next to Astrid's name. I didn't want it to be her. Not remotely.

I looked over my list and took a deep breath, feeling calmer now that I was taking some sort of action. Tomorrow morning, after everyone had left for breakfast, I was going to search Ivy's room for something concrete. I knew it was risky, but I didn't care. If I could prove that Ivy was the murderer, that she had been working to destroy me for months, at least I might actually be able to sleep at night. Then I could concentrate on earning Noelle's forgiveness for what I'd done, getting back into Billings, and maybe even winning Josh back too.

I could concentrate on reclaiming my life.

"Thank you so much for fixing my computer last night," Jillian said as she and Ivy walked out of their room on Monday morning. I listened from the other side of my door, my breath coming quick and shallow. "I thought the thing was fritzed, and I totally forgot to back up my world civ paper."

"Not a problem," Ivy replied. They were in the hallway now, passing just outside my door. "But how many times have I told you, *always* back up *everything*?"

"I know, I know, Bill Gates," Jillian said with a laugh. "I promise I will never again question your computer geek ways."

"I prefer computer diva," Ivy joked.

I closed my eyes as a wave of realization came over me. Ivy, a computer geek? No wonder she'd been able to rig Cheyenne's e-mail to keep sending me that suicide note over and over and over again. No wonder she'd been able to get through to my accounts no matter how I tried to block her or how many times I changed my address. The more I learned about the girl, the more certain I was that she was my tormentor. I made a mental note to add this new bit of info to my suspect list.

The moment I heard the elevator ping and Ivy and Jillian's laughter fade, I slipped out of my room. It was getting late, and the hallway was deserted. Taking a deep breath and saying a quick prayer that Ivy and Jillian wouldn't double back for anything, I grasped the cold bronze doorknob and pushed. Ten million times I had cursed the powers that be for deciding we didn't need locks on our dorm room doors. For once, I couldn't have been more grateful.

Ivy and Jillian's room was about twice the size of mine, and they had made it cozy by draping colorful scarves across the ceiling to hide the ugly stucco. The walls were papered with full-size posters, magazine tear sheets, and framed photographs; not an inch of graying white paint peeked through anywhere. Their beds, pushed against opposite walls, were littered with throw pillows, and their desks stood back-to-back in front of the window so that they could both see out when they were studying. And so that they couldn't see each other and get distracted. Not a bad little system. I'd have to remember that if I ever had a roommate again.

Okay. What was I doing? This was not an episode of *Pimp My Dorm*. I was here for information.

Glancing around, I identified Ivy's side of the room by a square frame holding a photo of her and Josh, clearly taken out on the quad. They were smiling and hugging.

Gag, heave, gag.

Part of me wanted to smash it, burn it, tear it to shreds, but instead I quickly sifted through a short stack of papers next to her computer. It was all college brochures and copies of the applications she'd sent: Harvard, Dartmouth, Tufts, Wesleyan, Boston College. Clearly the girl wanted to stay close to home. I yanked open the first drawer of her desk. Nothing but pens, pencils, pads, and printer ink. The second drawer was all old notebooks, which I paged through quickly, finding nothing interesting other than a couple of doodled hearts with Ivy's and Gage's names in them. Ew.

Why hadn't those two just stayed together? They were so perversely well-suited for each other.

The bottom drawer of her desk was filled with snack food and feminine products. A weird combination, but I had a hunch it wouldn't be of interest to Detective Hauer or Josh.

I stood up and looked around. Only the dresser and closet were left, and I was getting tenser with each passing second. There had to be something here. Something . . .

And that was when my eyes found the photo. Hanging on the wall above Ivy's bed was a full-color, eight-by-ten picture of four girls with their arms draped around one another. It wouldn't have been remotely out of the ordinary, if not for the totally eerie and creepy lineup. Ivy was on one end, then Cheyenne, then Noelle, then Ariana.

A killer, a victim, a friend, and a killer.

Just looking at Ariana's openly smiling face gave me chills, and I had to turn away. The girl had tried to murder me. Had succeeded in killing Thomas Pearson. Why would anyone want a picture of her up in their room, let alone Ivy—the girl who had told me she hated Ariana and Noelle above anyone? It just didn't add up.

Steeling myself, I studied the photo, looking for clues. Judging by the girls' clothes and the blossoming tree behind them, the picture had been taken in the spring, but when? Why? Why those four and only those four? I was about to pluck the photo off the wall for a closer look, when down the hallway a door slammed, scaring the breath right out of me. My head whipped around to look at the door and I took a few stumbling steps away from the bed, every inch of me shaking. I couldn't stay here any longer. I was going to have to continue my search another time.

As I fumbled with the doorknob, I took one last look at the photo. Why on earth would Ivy want the faces of the people who had betrayed her to be the last thing she saw before closing her eyes at night?

There was definitely something freaky going on here. And I was going to figure out what it was.

SUSPECT NUMERO UNO

I skipped breakfast, spending the hour calming my nerves, adding to my list of evidence against Ivy, and sending Noelle an e-mail apologizing once again for what I had done. All I could do was hope that she would have an unguarded moment and read the message, and that my words might start to melt the ice wall she had put up between us. I finally headed out in time to make it to morning services at the chapel, where I sneaked in at the back of the crowd.

The vibe in the air was hushed, paranoid. Apparently everyone had heard about the murder investigation at breakfast. And if they hadn't, the two uniformed cops stationed near the doors of the chapel certainly set an eerie tone.

". . . police are taking over Dean Marcus's old office. . . ."

"Are they going to interrogate *everyone?* I didn't even know the girl."

". . . everyone knows who did it anyway—"

When I heard that one, my head whipped around, but I couldn't
tell who had said it. I was soon bustled right down the center aisle to
the junior section, where I was about to sit in my usual pew—until I
realized it was a Billings pew. Instead, I took the one two rows back
and tried to hold my head high.

"Hi, Reed," Constance whispered as she slid into the pew in front
of mine. "How was your first night in your new room?" she asked, trying to sound all positive and upbeat.

"Fine," I lied, the back of my neck flushed with heat. I could
practically feel Noelle watching us from a few rows back. I knew she
wouldn't like the idea of Constance fraternizing with the enemy. "But
the room itself is kind of dark and depressing."

"I missed you," Sabine added as she joined Constance. "It was so
odd, sleeping in that room alone."

A lump of sorrow filled my throat, nearly choking me. Meanwhile,
Missy shot me a death glare as she, Lorna, Astrid, and Kiki filed in
next to Sabine.

"You guys better quit it," Missy hissed to my friends while glancing
at me. "Noelle will eat you alive for talking to her."

My heart squeezed tightly in my chest.

"I don't care what Noelle thinks," Sabine said defiantly.

"No, you guys, Missy's right," I said, as much as it pained me to
agree with her. "You don't want to get on her bad side right now. I'm
fine. Just . . . face forward."

Constance and Sabine turned their backs to me reluctantly and I
slumped against the hard pew. A few other juniors filled in the seats

to my right, all eyeing me with curiosity, wondering why I was in their row. I supposed the news of my expulsion from Billings hadn't completely made the rounds yet. Either that or they were still obsessing over the Reed-and-Dash-seminude show they had all gotten to see. I had been the subject of whispers and stares ever since the night of the fund-raiser.

"Good morning, faculty and students of Easton Academy!" Headmaster Cromwell announced, taking his spot behind the podium.

"Good morning, Headmaster Cromwell," we dutifully recited.

With a nod, our fearless leader got right down to the morning announcements. He wore a gray suit and blue tie this morning, along with his ever-present American flag tie tack. His white hair was perfectly slicked back from his face and his voice boomed throughout the chapel as always, but I noticed something different about him. There was something almost jaunty in the way he spoke and held his head. Like Mr. Serious was actually excited about something.

How was that possible, when we had another murder on our hands and the Easton Police Department taking over offices in Hell Hall so they could question students?"And now, a final announcement that I'm hoping will bring a bit of levity to our lives here at Easton," he said, looking across the room. A never-before-seen sparkle danced in his normally dead blue eyes. "This year I have decided to reinstate an old Easton Academy tradition—the Easton Academy Holiday Dinner."

Instantly, the entire chapel filled with an excited buzz. Everyone, it seemed, knew what this dinner was—all except me.

"For those of you who are new to our community, the Easton Academy Holiday Dinner is a catered banquet held in the dining hall. There will be traditional holiday fair and decorations, the Easton Academy Chorale will treat us to a holiday concert, and everyone will have a chance to relax and unwind before finals. All students and faculty are invited. In my day this dinner was the social event of the season. I'm hoping it will be that again."

The buzzing intensified as the girls around me started gabbing about how their mothers and grandmothers had always talked about the Holiday Dinner and how fabulous it was. I was surprised my classmates could get so excited about a dinner in the cafeteria.

"The dinner will be held next Friday night. Dress will be formal," the headmaster continued. "Also, each student will be receiving a special note in his or her mailbox this afternoon. This note will contain the name of another Easton student. You are to select a gift for this student and bring it, wrapped in holiday paper, to the dinner, to be placed under the Easton tree."

"Yay! Presents!" Lorna said, clapping her hands. "I hope someone good gets me."

Now the talking was at an all-time high. Headmaster Cromwell raised his large hands and called for silence. Instantly, the chapel went quiet. We were all used to following his demands by now.

"Finally," he said, "the Holiday Dinner also includes a toasting hour, one of my favorite traditions. During this hour any student who wishes to do so will have the opportunity to stand up and toast another member of the Easton community, whether it be for their service to

the school or their academic achievement or their steadfast friendship. It is an honor to be singled out during toasting hour, so if you
intend to speak for someone, please prepare your toast in advance.
Your speeches should be eloquent and from the heart. Anyone giving
an inappropriate speech will, of course, be dealt with accordingly.
That is all."

"Leave it to Cromwell to end on a sour note," Lorna said under her
breath.

Still, everyone around me was chatting happily, and smiles
abounded. I couldn't help thinking that, for once, the Crom had gotten it right. This dinner was exactly what Easton needed. Something
to look forward to. Something to get our minds off Cheyenne's murder investigation.

As soon as we were dismissed, I jumped up and exited the
chapel as fast as I could. Outside, the bright sun bounced off the
white blanket of snow covering the quad, nearly blinding me. I
had to close my eyes for a split second, and my foot came down
on someone else's. Blinking, I could just make out the purple-y
shadow of Amberly Carmichael, freshman and heir to the Coffee
Carma empire. I was just opening my mouth to apologize when she
cut me off.

"Watch it," she snapped, yanking a white wool cap over her wavy
blond hair. "I don't want to be your next victim."

Her two sidekicks, who always hovered behind her, laughed before
they all sauntered off. For a second, I didn't move. I was too stunned.
Since when did Amberly talk to me that way? Since when did any

freshman talk to any upperclassman that way? And next victim? What was that about?

I looked around at the crowd still pouring through the doors. Several people who had been looking at me looked away, and a few sophomore girls hanging out near the outer wall of the chapel sneered in my direction. I saw Detective Hauer coming my way with a uniformed police officer and my pulse froze in my veins.

Please. Not here.

They walked right by me. But that was when I heard the whispers.

"That's her."

"She totally did it."

". . . capable of anything."

"Psycho whore, basically. That's what we should call her."

My heartbeat pounded in every inch of my body. These weren't the same scathing remarks I'd been getting before Thanksgiving break. These were worse. Venomous. What was going on?

Just then Gage Coolidge slipped through the chapel doors and started past me. My hand shot out, grabbing his leather-clad arm.

Gage paused, looked down at my hand like it was a leech, and slowly pulled his arm away. He dusted off his designer coat like I'd left a trail of ants behind.

"Not cool," he said, looking past me. His handsome face was ruddy from the cold and his eyes darted around as if concerned about who might see us together.

"Don't worry. This'll only take a second," I said, bravely squaring my shoulders. If there was anyone on this campus who had no right to judge someone else based on their sexual escapades, it was Gage. Plus, he had always been brutally honest. It was one of the only things I liked about him. And hated, depending on the situation. "What the hell is going on? Everyone's looking at me like I'm about to blow up the building."

"Funny!" Gage said. "Amazing how you can be funny right now, Brennan. They must've raised you tough out on the farm."

I grabbed his arm again and pulled him around the corner, away from the prying eyes of the crowd. "What are they saying about me now?"

Gage scoffed, his head tipping back as he did so. "What *aren't* they saying? Rumor has it that you were the one who got dragged in for questioning before break. Apparently *you* are suspect numero uno in Cheyenne's murder."

"What?" I breathed.

"Good surprise face, kid. I like a girl who can act," Gage said, amused.

"I'm not acting, idiot," I replied. "Yeah, Hauer questioned me, but that was before they even knew for sure she was murdered. And I am not a suspect."

"That's not what everyone's saying. They're saying you offed Cheyenne so that Noelle could get back into Billings," Gage reported bluntly. He reached up to smooth his short, brown hair forward, rolling his eyes skyward as if he could see what he was doing.

"That again?" I said, throwing up my hands and letting them slap down at my sides. "Noelle quashed that one a couple weeks ago."

"Yeah, well, it's back. Only no one thinks Noelle was involved anymore," Gage informed me. Apparently satisfied with his coif now, he shoved his ungloved hands under his arms to keep them warm. "They're saying you couldn't stand not having Noelle down the hall from you because you worship her so hard-core, so you forced Cheyenne to take those pills and forged the suicide note. They're also saying that having Noelle in Billings wasn't enough. You wanted to *be* Noelle, and that's why you got all horizontal with her boyfriend."

My brain couldn't process this information. It was bad enough being looked upon as a backstabbing slut. Now everyone thought I was a murderer, too? I glanced around at the few people walking along the path to the library and once again, every last one of them quickly looked away.

"Was it because you didn't get enough love out there in East Bumblefart, Pennsylvania?" Gage asked, his voice dripping with false sympathy. "Is that why you do the things you do, Brennan?"

"I didn't do anything," I said through my teeth, my fingers clenching into fists. "Cheyenne was leaving anyway—she was expelled."

"Yeah. You just keep telling yourself that," Gage said. "You know, if the world isn't giving you enough hugs, you can always hug yourself," he said mockingly, crossing his arms in an X over his chest with a sad little frown. Then he laughed and strode away with his signature swagger.

I stood there for a moment in shock, unable to move or think or breathe. Noelle was the only person who knew I had been the one to be questioned by Hauer that night. Why would she do this? Why would she start such a vicious rumor? Hadn't I been through enough already?

Unless she was trying to send me a message. Trying to tell me how very over we actually were. This wasn't something you did to a person you planned to eventually forgive. This was something you did to a person you hated to her very core.

My eyes filled with hot tears. Noelle hated me. She really and truly hated me.

A few girls from Pemberly walked by and saw me standing there, looking like I'd just been told I had three days to live. They all clutched each other and moved quickly away, like they thought I might suddenly attack. On their retreat they nearly ran over Josh Hollis and Ivy Slade. My boyfriend and my stalker. My boyfriend and the murderer.

My whole body went numb at the sight of Josh. His dark blond curls danced in the wind, and his blue eyes looked pained as he passed by me, like he wanted to talk. Almost like he was *desperate* to talk to me. But then Ivy tightened her grip on his arm and he turned away, ducking through the door to Hull Hall.

That was it. It was all I could take. I shoved my notebook into my bag and took off for class alone.

INSIGNIFICANT

I survived that first day back by focusing on my teachers when I was in class and keeping my head down and my earbuds in when I wasn't. At lunch I grabbed a sandwich and ate it by myself outside in the frigid air. Dinner I skipped entirely. Basically I played right into my new role—that of campus outcast extraordinaire.

But after another sleepless night, I realized I couldn't live like this. First, I loved breakfast. Pretty much lived for it, actually. And second, I didn't want to prove everyone right. I couldn't slink around campus and let them think I was guilty. I *hated* proving people right. From that morning on I was going to hold my head high. People could say what they wanted. It wasn't going to affect me.

Besides, I wanted to keep an eye on Ivy whenever I could. Who knew when she might trip up and give something away? I wanted to be there when it happened.

Of course, when I emerged from the breakfast line on Tuesday

morning I immediately doubted the sagacity of my plan. My
eyes instinctively darted to the Billings tables and I felt such an
instant and intense longing I almost fell over. There they were.
My old friends. Looking as beautiful and untouchable as ever.
They laughed and chatted and passed around holiday catalogs and
checked out one another's notes for class. Somehow, they seemed
even more stylish and alluring and perfect than usual. Like when
Josh had miraculously woken up even hotter the day after we'd
broken up.

I forced myself to look at the other tables and seek out some new
place to sit. But only wary, suspicious faces greeted me.

What was I thinking? This was never going to work. There was
nowhere for me to go.

"Hey, Reed."

I flinched, startled that someone was actually talking to me. When
I turned around I found Diana Waters, Kiki's roommate in Bradwell
last year, hovering behind me. Behind her were two of her friends
from Pemberly—Sonal Shah and Shane Freundel, people I knew
vaguely from class. I had noticed Diana hanging out with them ever
since Kiki had been invited to live in Billings.

"Hi, Diana," I said. "Hey," I added to the girls behind her. They
gaped at me as if amazed I possessed the ability to speak.

"You can sit with us, if you want," Diana offered, a smile lighting
up her pretty, makeup-free face. She pushed a blond wave off her
shoulder.

I was so relieved I could have hugged her, but at the same time some shallow part of my inner being felt exactly how far I had fallen. A couple of weeks ago I had basically been the queen of this place. I'd had the most sought-after guys falling all over each other to ask me out and all the most elite girls at Easton hanging on my every word. Now a group of lowly Pemberly juniors in jeans, hoodies, and sneakers were extending a pity invite to their breakfast table. I could only imagine the giggles Noelle would get out of this.

Still, it was better than eating alone.

"Thanks," I said.

I managed to keep my chin up as I followed them to their table in the far wing, away from the center of the room where the Billings Girls held court. I refused to look to see if Noelle and the others were watching. Wouldn't give them the satisfaction. But I felt as if I were under a harsh spotlight as I walked, and when I finally fell into a chair at Diana's table, I felt exhausted.

"Nice table," I said, forcing a smile for Diana and her friends. "Very private."

They all smiled in a self-conscious way, but no one replied. Ooookay.

Trying to act as if everything was perfectly normal, I picked up my bottle of apple juice, shook it up, and popped the top. As I took a sip, I realized that Diana and her two friends were all communicating with one another silently, darting looks and nudging shoulders. Sour apprehension filled my stomach.

"What?" I said, lowering the bottle.

"You didn't actually kill Cheyenne Martin, right?" Sonal asked. She was big-boned with dark skin and black curly hair and had a slight Hindi accent. Her dark eyes were wide behind her glasses.

"Sonal! God!" Diana said with a scoff, her cheeks turning pink. She shot me an apologetic look as she buttered her bagel. "Of course Reed didn't."

"No, of course I didn't," I echoed quietly.

This seemed to appease both Sonal and Shane. I saw their shoulders visibly relax.

"So, what's it like to live in Billings?" Shane asked, crunching into an apple. The juice sprayed all over the place. She was a tall, athletic type with plain brown hair and plain brown eyes.

My heart twisted at the question. "It's . . . uh . . ."

"Is it true you each have your own personal maid?" Sonal asked, scooting forward in her chair.

"No. Where did you hear—"

"But you do get an allowance every week from the alumni, right?" Shane asked. "Everyone knows that."

"Well, not exactly. We don't—"

"Do you guys really have champagne parties every Friday night?" Sonal demanded. "I mean, *did* you? And were guys really allowed to come?"

"Yeah. That one's true," I said. "Except for the guys . . ."

I glanced over at the Billings tables again and paused. Noelle, who always sat near the edge of the table, had several boxes and gift bags piled around her feet. Portia and the Twin Cities were pawing through a huge gift basket filled with Fekkai hair products and M.A.C. makeup and Bliss Spa essentials in the center of the table. As I watched, a steady stream of junior and senior girls stopped by the table to chat, each offering some kind of gift.

"That's weird," I said under my breath.

"What?" Diana asked, glancing over.

"It's a little early for Christmas gifts, isn't it?" I said.

"Oh, those aren't Christmas gifts," Sonal said, shaking some salt over her scrambled eggs.

"You haven't heard?" Diana appeared confused.

I instantly got that tight feeling around my heart. The one I get whenever everyone knows something I don't.

"Heard what?" I asked.

"Everyone's been talking about it since yesterday morning," Diana said, taking a bite of her bagel. "They're looking for someone to—"

She stopped midsentence and looked at me guiltily. I felt as if someone had just yanked my chair out from under my butt.

"Someone to replace me," I finished. Slowly, I pushed my tray of pancakes away, no longer hungry.

"I'm sorry. I still can't believe they threw you out," Sonal said, her eyes wide but her voice quiet. "I mean, you were the president!"

"Yeah . . . ," I said. There was a lump lodged in my windpipe, even though I'd yet to eat a thing. "So . . . why aren't you all over there trying to bribe your way in?" I asked, trying to lighten the mood. "Don't you guys want to be in Billings?"

"Not really," Diana said, scrunching her nose.

I stared at her. Aside from Ivy, I'd never heard of a girl at Easton not wanting to be in Billings.

"Why not?" I asked.

Diana looked around at her friends and shrugged. "We kind of like it where we are. It may seem boring to you guys, but at least we don't have to deal with all the drama."

"We have other priorities," Shane added with a sniff. "Like, other than shopping."

Okay, ouch. This one at least had the requisite Billings bitchiness down.

"But that doesn't mean we're not curious about it," Sonal said, wiping her fingers on her napkin. "So. Tell us. If you didn't kill Cheyenne, then who do you think did?"

"Sonal!" Diana scolded again.

That was about as much as I could take. I pushed myself up from my chair.

"I have to go," I said.

"Reed, I'm sorry. You don't have to—"

"No. It's cool. Thanks, Diana," I said. "I'll see you in class."

I grabbed my coat and bag and turned around, looking forward to a speedy exit into the cold air outside. Just as I was about to push through the back door of the caf, I almost walked into Amberly Carmichael for the second time in as many days. For once she was making an appearance sans her normally hovering friends. Her wavy blond hair was back in a velvet headband and she wore a long tweed skirt over black leather boots. In her arms was a Tiffany box that was half the size of a cafeteria table, a box she'd come close to dropping during our near collision.

"Hey!" she snapped loudly, looking me up and down. "You break it, you buy it."

"Sorry," I said, not meaning it.

She sighed, rolling her big blue eyes, and placed the box down on the empty table next to us.

"Actually, I'm glad you almost bumped into me," she said loudly, tugging her leather gloves off finger by finger. "I'll be needing that Carma Card back."

Half the cafeteria fell silent, all the better to eavesdrop. I looked around, my face turning ten shades of red. From the corner of my eye, I saw Portia and Shelby craning their necks to better see the proceedings. Noelle was looking on, amused. Clearly Amberly was performing for them. This little twit who had been kowtowing to me since the beginning of the year. The girl who would have jumped off a bridge if I'd asked her to a week ago. Now she was treating me like the hired help. Or worse. Could this be any more humiliating?

Yes, I realized, it could. If I gave the stupid piece of plastic back to her.

"Right. Like that's gonna happen," I said, tilting my head and trying for my best superior Billings Girl tone. I started by her, but she quickly stepped in front of me.

"You're not keeping it," she said with a condescending laugh. "I gave it to you. I can take it back."

All the guys sitting two tables down were watching me mirthfully, waiting for my breakdown. And why not? What formerly powerful junior wouldn't break down in the face of defiance from a scrawny freshman? In fact, most of the people in the room were watching me with that anticipation in their eyes. I felt myself start to crumble as giggles and snickers surrounded me, but then I saw Josh and Ivy stroll through the door hand in hand. Together they paused, instantly noting the big spotlight on my forehead. That was all I needed. No way were those two going to see me go down. And given that I had handled the disc showdown with Noelle, I could certainly deal with Amberly.

"Manners, Amberly," I said, *tsk*ing under my breath. "Didn't your parents ever teach you it's impolite to rescind a gift?"

Her eyes searched mine for a moment, uncertain. Apparently this comment had somehow hit home. Guess her parents *were* big on propriety.

"Plus, I want to keep it as a souvenir. Maybe it'll be a collector's item after Starbucks finally destroys your dad's business," I said.

The guys at the nearest table let out a long, low "oooooh," and I couldn't help but smile. Finally, score one for me. Amberly's face turned bright red and I took the opportunity to shoulder my bag and skirt by her. I slipped right past Josh and Ivy and beelined for the door, savoring my triumph. Savoring the fact that I was still capable of having one. That maybe everything wasn't quite as hopeless as I'd thought.

S.O.

That afternoon Sabine, Diana, and I sat on one of the benches on the quad, going over the history reading. It was a bizarrely warm day for December, and melting ice and snow dripped from the stone buildings' rooftops into the gutter catches below. Most of Easton was taking advantage of the anomalous weather, and the quad was dotted with klatches of students, many of whom were clearly gossiping about me, of course. They kept throwing me curious looks, tilting their heads together and whispering. I couldn't believe that Sabine and Diana were so willing to risk being seen with the school pariah.

"Doesn't it bother you that everyone's staring at us?" I finally asked.

Diana glanced up from her textbook. "Are they? I didn't notice."

"Doesn't bother me at all," Sabine replied with a shrug.

I grinned, touched again by Sabine's unwavering friendship. And how had I never realized how unabashedly nice Diana was? Oh, right.

Because I had always been too busy trying to get in with the Billings Girls.

"Do you think he's going to give us a pop quiz? Because if he does, he's definitely going to ask about all these stupid baby boom statistics," Diana said, pointing at a bulleted list in the book. "Barber just *loves* to talk about the baby boomers."

I was about to focus—I really was—but then I saw Trey Prescott, Josh's roommate, walking by with some books tucked under his arm. Immediately I started to wonder—what did Trey think of Ivy? He had to know more about her and Josh's relationship than I did. They probably spent all kinds of time in Josh and Trey's room together. Had Trey ever heard her say anything weird or seen her act erratically? Suddenly, I had to know. And Trey was, atypically, alone, which was a blessing for me. He was a lot more likely to talk to me if he was alone. Feeling a sudden flutter of nerves, I jumped up and grabbed my bag.

"I have to go. Sorry," I said to Diana and Sabine. "But yeah. He's definitely going to ask about the baby boomers."

I took off after Trey, ignoring the baffled expressions on my friends' faces, and caught up to him right at the base of the library steps.

"Trey!" I called out.

He paused and turned around. He was wearing a thick white turtleneck sweater that set off the dark color of his skin, and he'd recently had his black hair shorn so close to his scalp that it was barely there. Trey was widely considered to be one of the hottest, sweetest, and most mature guys at Easton. Why Cheyenne had ever let him go, I had no idea. Somehow, he didn't seem surprised to see me jogging toward him. Even better, he didn't look remotely annoyed or disturbed by my presence.

"Hey, Reed. What's up?" he asked. He casually held his books with both hands down at waist level in front of him and looked me in the eye. "How're you doing?" he asked in a low voice.

"I'm fine," I said, catching my breath. "Well, you know, not really, but—"

"I can imagine you pretty much want to blow this joint," he said, shaking his head at my gawkers. "Bunch of losers."

"So . . . you don't believe the rumor?" I asked tentatively, walking over to lean back against one of the metal handrails leading up to the library.

Trey scoffed and joined me, leaning next to me. "Please. You didn't kill Cheyenne any more than I did."

I winced. Little did he know, his name was on the list of potential suspects tucked into my book bag. Not that I really believed he'd done it, but still.

"The whole Dash thing, however . . ." He looked at me admonishingly. "Let's just not go there."

"Fair enough," I replied, hugging myself against a sudden chill. Trey and Josh had become seriously close friends this year, so the last subject I wanted to broach with Trey was his feelings on my infamous slut video.

"So what's up?" he asked.

"Actually, I was just kind of wondering . . ."

How the hell was I going to say this? I realized, suddenly, what a loser I was going to look like, asking about my ex's new girlfriend. But it wasn't because I was pathetically lovesick—it was because I suspected the girl of murder.

Trey's brow creased and he looked at me with those warm brown eyes of his. "Wondering what?"

Okay, Reed. Just ask him.

"What do you think of Ivy?" I blurted.

Trey stared at me for a second, then laughed, bringing the side of his fist to his mouth. He pushed away from the railing. "Oh, come on. You're not really asking me that, are you? I would have thought you were above that whole jealous ex-girlfriend thing."

"I'm not asking as a jealous ex-girlfriend," I told him, my face burning. "It's not like I want Josh back."

Even though I do.

"Oh, really?" Trey said, his eyes dancing. "Then why are you asking?"

I took a deep breath and waited for a pair of guys from Drake to lumber their way up the stairs to the library doors. "I think she might have killed Cheyenne," I whispered.

At this, all the mirth dropped away from Trey's face. "What?"

"It's just a theory right now," I explained. "I'm trying to gather information—"

"No. There's no way," Trey said, shaking his head. "Those two used to be best friends. Ivy would never have hurt Cheyenne."

"You don't think?" I asked. "Even after their . . . falling-out?"

"No way." Trey was adamant. Which, considering how convinced

I was, kind of got under my skin. He leaned back next to me again. "Sorry, Nancy Drew. I think you're way off on this one. Even though they were hanging out with different crowds when Cheyenne died, I think there was always a connection between them, you know?"

I didn't know what to say . . . what to ask. I had been so sure that he would agree with me on some level that I was totally thrown. Trey looked down at the concrete steps and pushed at a wilted brown leaf with the toe of his boot.

"I still can't even believe this is happening," he mused quietly. "I mean, it's psychotic, thinking that someone on this campus might have killed her." He glanced sidelong at me and adjusted his books. "Would you believe the cops have questioned me five times already?"

I blinked, stunned. "Five times? Why?"

"I *am* the ex-boyfriend," Trey reminded me, lifting his shoulders. "Cops love that shit."

"Right."

"Luckily I have an airtight alibi," he said. "So they finally gave up."

"Really?" I asked, trying to sound like a moderately interested friend, rather than a person who had anything riding on said alibi. But suddenly all I could think about was how happy I would be to officially cross Trey off the suspect list. "What is it?"

Trey took a deep breath and looked out across the evergreen bushes that lined the steps. "Well, actually, Josh was having a hard time sleeping, you know, after you and he . . ."

I gulped in some cool air and tried to ignore the tightness in my chest. "We'd broken up around then."

"Right," Trey said, rubbing the back of his neck with one hand. "So I was trying to help the guy out, you know? Distract him and all. We were up pretty much all night trying to beat these suckers from Malaysia on Infinite Warrior. Guys were in and out of our room all night, cheering us on, eating our food. Plus there's the site you have to link to so you can play internationally. They have a log of how long we were playing. Which was, unfortunately, way too long."

He laughed in a self-deprecating way and I let out a sigh of relief. I wasn't sure if I could handle being so very wrong about a friend again. The Ariana thing had been bad enough.

"So, anyway, sorry to burst your bubble about Ivy, but I've known the girl since freshman year. I really don't see it happening," he said, standing up straight.

Yeah, well, no one had seen the Ariana thing coming either, had they? Just because Trey thought Ivy was innocent . . . that didn't make her innocent.

"I'll see you around," he said, lifting his chin.

"Yeah. See ya."

Trey started up the stairs to the library, then paused, his shoes scraping on the wet concrete steps. He turned and looked down at me from a few steps up.

"There is one thing. I told the police, so I guess it won't hurt to tell you," he said.

"What's that?" I asked, intrigued.

"I'm pretty sure Cheyenne was cheating on me last spring," he said, a slight blush coming to his cheeks.

"Dominic Infante?" I suggested before I could check myself.

Dominic was a guy I had gone on one date with in New York City. He'd gotten insanely drunk and confessed that he'd slept with Cheyenne several times before her death.

Trey laughed. "No. She didn't hook up with him until this September, I don't think. No, it was someone else. She used to get these texts all the time from someone with the initials S.O. and she'd get all flustered and weird about them. Finally one day I snagged her phone and checked out the texts and they seemed totally innocent, but the way she acted when they came in . . . I don't know. It wasn't right."

I smirked. "You checked her texts?"

"Hey. Nobody's perfect," Trey said, spreading his arms wide.

As he jogged up the steps and disappeared into the library, my mind scrolled through all the people I'd ever met or even heard of, searching for an S.O. Of course it came up blank. But at least I now had something new to go on. Maybe the answer to all my problems would be as easy as IDing S.O.

As I walked into the post office that afternoon, Jason Darlington was walking out. I automatically opened my mouth to say hi—we were in the same English class and we'd hung out before the Billings fundraiser debacle. He automatically went to hold the door. But when he saw it was me, his normally friendly face shut down entirely and he let the heavy door slam closed behind him. If not for my catlike reflexes, I would have been crushed.

Guess that was one more person who wasn't talking to me.

Trying to ignore the ever-growing hole in my heart, I swung the door wide and walked inside. The post office was jam-packed with chatting students, the excitement in the air palpable. They were all holding little blue cards and passing them around to check out the names they contained. Everyone was there for the same reason I was: to find out who they would be gifting at the Holiday Dinner.

Steeling myself for another wave of glares, stares, and whispers,

I rolled my shoulders back and wove through the crowd. Sudden pockets of silence followed me all the way to my box. I thought back to the way the campus had felt after we had all heard about Thomas's murder last year. How eerie it was, with everyone wondering who among us might be a murderer. But this felt totally different, because this time everyone had already decided it was me. So instead of an eerie vibe, there was more of a growing sense of animosity toward me. A focused, sizzling, unifying hatred—like eventually, these people might organize and decide it was time to take me down.

Let's just say it did not feel good. My face was giving off as much heat as the summer sun, but I managed to shake my hair back and concentrate on opening my mailbox's lock. Sooner or later I would clear my name and these people would all have to apologize for suspecting me. For now it was get in and get out. That was the plan.

Then someone stepped up to a box a few feet away from mine and I could feel whoever it was eyeing me tentatively. Against my own will, I glanced over. It was Marc Alberro. My date for the Billings fundraiser who hadn't spoken to me once since dismissing me that night. He approached me slowly, letting his dark hair fall over his forehead as if he was trying to hide. My heart fluttered with nervousness. Not that I cared all that much what Marc Alberro thought of me, but would this be another public call-out? God, I hoped not.

"Hey, Reed. What's up?" he asked. His tone was conciliatory, which relaxed my tense shoulders a bit.

"Oh, I think we all know what's up," I replied, glancing at a group of girls who were eyeing me nearby. "What's up with you? I thought you were never going to speak to me again after the fund-raiser."

I suppose I shouldn't have been surprised when Marc basically told me to walk away after the Dash video had been zapped to everyone we knew. He was, after all, a decent guy and a member of Easton's Purity Club. A guy like that would definitely not be happy about everyone seeing his date's sloppy hookup with another guy. Another girl's guy, to be exact. I already had two strikes against me, so why was he talking to me now? Wasn't an alleged murder rap strike three?

"Yeah, well, I've thought about it a lot and . . . when it comes down to it, it's not really my business what you did before we met," he said quietly, leaning back against the wall of P.O. boxes. "It's not even really my business what you've done since."

His words made me feel both chagrined and relieved at the same time. He was telling me he no longer had any interest in going out with me. Which, while it was a rejection, was kind of a welcome rejection. With everything else that was going on right then, the last thing I needed was to navigate the murky waters of a new relationship. Especially one I hadn't been all that into to begin with. Marc was a nice guy and all—smart, cute, funny—but I had never felt that thing you're supposed to feel when you like a guy. That "I might die if I don't see him again before the next class" thing. That thing I always had with Josh.

"So . . . friends?" I said.

Marc smiled, his whole face lighting up. What? Had he expected me to make a scene? "Friends."

"Cool."

I smiled, possibly my first real smile of the last two days, and opened my mailbox. Inside was the same little blue card everyone else had received. I pulled it out and flipped it over.

JOSHUA HOLLIS, KETLAR, SENIOR

"You have to be kidding me," I said aloud. Why didn't they just saddle me with Ivy Slade, too?

"What? Who'd you get?" Marc asked, leaning over.

I turned the card for him to see and he whistled under his breath.

"Someone in Hell Hall has a twisted sense of humor," he said.

I slammed the tiny metal door shut and stuffed the card into the back pocket of my jeans. "I'm starting to think this entire school has a twisted sense of humor."

Marc glanced at our gaggle of onlookers. I saw Amberly's two side-kicks checking me out, but they both blushed and looked away the second I caught them, pretending to be absorbed in the new Barneys catalog. "I know what you mean. Come on."

He grabbed my hand and led me through the crowd, cutting a path so I wouldn't have to be there any longer than absolutely necessary. As soon as we were back outside in the cool evening air, I gulped in a deep breath.

"Thanks."

"No problem. I seriously can't believe anyone thinks you would have hurt Cheyenne," Marc said, shaking his head. "I mean, just because a person makes a sex tape, that doesn't mean they're capable of murder."

My face flushed crimson. "I didn't make a sex tape. Someone did that without me knowing. And by the way, there was no actual sex involved."

"Well, in any case," Marc said as we started across the quad, "I bet there are at least fifty suspects who make more sense than you do. I mean, the girl was always juggling two or three guys at a time. Maybe one of *them* finally snapped. A crime of passion makes a lot more sense than someone killing for a spot in a dorm."

A warm, tingling rush came over me and I paused. That rush you get when you suddenly realize that someone has said something important. Maybe something they didn't mean to say.

"Wait a minute. How do you know she was juggling several guys at a time?" I asked.

Marc stopped walking, already a couple of feet ahead of me, but it took a second for him to turn around. A long second. Every inch of my skin was on fire. This wasn't the first time Marc had blurted something about Cheyenne that he'd had no real reason for knowing. He had also brought up the whole Cheyenne-drugging-Josh thing a couple of weeks ago.

"Just something I heard," he replied with a shrug, looking me in the eye. His expression bordered on defiant.

"Kind of like everyone's now heard I killed Cheyenne," I said pointedly. "How do you know it wasn't just a rumor?"

"Well, let's just say this one I had on good authority," Marc replied with a smirk. "Anyway, I should be getting to the paper. I have a couple of stories to polish before we put it to bed."

He turned and speed-walked away so fast, I didn't even have time to formulate another question, let alone a good-bye.

NEW HOME

I sat at my desk on Tuesday evening, listening to a Katy Rose CD and rereading the same gossip article about Ivy for the ten millionth time. It didn't matter how many times I Googled her, it was always the same articles. Mentions of her family's philanthropy, her grandmother's long obituary, some old piece about Ivy and her horse winning some random juniors competition years ago. Google wasn't about to explain that photo I had found in Ivy's room. It wasn't about to spit out a video of Ivy killing Cheyenne. All it was going to do was frustrate me.

Giving up for now, I slapped the laptop closed and turned around to look at my cavelike room. I hadn't put anything away yet. I think I was hoping that it wasn't real. Or maybe I just wasn't ready to give in. Stashing my clothes in that sad little dresser and tucking my bags under the creaky old bed would be like admitting defeat. But that night, as I looked around the dreary, confining space, I couldn't take it anymore. I couldn't live in a bare cell, plucking my clothes out of suitcases all wrinkled like some kind of vagabond. It was too depressing. It might just send me over the edge.

Slowly, reluctantly, I pushed myself out of my chair and started to unpack my suitcase. Of course, right on top was the black cashmere sweater Noelle had given me on her return to Easton this fall. Just looking at it made my spirits plummet even further. Maybe this was not the best idea.

There was a quick knock at my door.

"Who is it?" I called out.

"Surprise!"

It was Constance and Sabine, and they had come bearing gifts.

"What're you guys doing here?" I asked, still clutching the sweater. I reached over to my CD player and turned the volume almost all the way down.

"You said your room was depressing, so we brought you some things to cheer the place up!" Sabine announced, walking in and placing a mini Christmas tree atop my dresser. She unfurled a bright red woven rug in the center of the floor. It just fit between the bed and the dresser.

"I picked out the posters," Constance said, holding up a cardboard tube. "I remembered you really liked Turner's seascapes in art history last year, so I ordered you a few prints and had them shipped overnight."

"Wow. Thanks, you guys. This is incredible," I said, taking the tube from Constance. Tears of gratitude actually welled in my eyes. They had come at the perfect time. "You didn't have to do this."

"Yeah, we did. Look at this place," Constance said, holding out both hands. Her face turned bright pink under her freckles. "I mean, not that it's bad. It's not. It's cozy, actually. I—"

"It's okay, Constance," I said, tossing the tube on my bed. "It's a hole."

"It's not a hole. In fact, I asked Headmaster Cromwell if I could transfer over here so we could be roommates again, but you were right. He wouldn't allow it since it's a single," Sabine said, smoothing out the corners of the rug.

I laughed, touched. "Well, at least you tried."

"Forget moving in here," Constance said, sitting down on my bed, which emitted its signature creak. She dropped her floral Betsey Johnson messenger bag next to her, spilling some of her books and notebooks halfway out. "What we really have to do is get you back into Billings."

"I second that," Sabine said, raising her hand. "But how?"

"Well, I was thinking," Constance said, sitting forward. She pulled her long, red braid over her shoulder and toyed with the piecey end. "You know how everyone who's trying to get into Billings is giving us gifts? Well, Reed, why don't you give Noelle something? Like a peace offering."

"Yes. It would be like telling her you want to start over from scratch," Sabine agreed, her green eyes excited.

"I don't know, you guys," I said, perching on the edge of my chair. "Wouldn't that seem kind of pathetic? And, you know, desperate?"

Constance's face fell into a pout. "I think it would be sweet."

"Maybe," I said, trying to bolster her. Looking at that face made me feel as if I'd just kicked a puppy. "I'll think about it."

"Good," Constance said. "Because I really think Noelle would respond to something like that."

Yeah. With a marathon laughing fit.

"We should put these up," Sabine suggested, reaching over for the posters. As she opened the tube and started unrolling the prints, I glanced at Constance's things and saw a copy of last week's *Easton Chronicle* sticking out of her bag. Instantly I thought of Marc and his odd comment earlier.

"Hey, Constance. You knew Marc last year, right?" I asked casually.

"Yeah. We met at the paper. Why?" Constance asked. She sat forward and turned the toes of her D&G sneakers together.

"Did he and Cheyenne ever hang out?" I asked.

"Not really," she said with a thoughtful frown. "But he *did* do a piece on her."

"He wrote a story about her?" I asked. That was unexpected.

"Yeah. Remember how we used to do that thing where we profiled a different student each week on page two?" Constance said. "I always thought it was kind of lame, so I cut it this year. But Marc wrote the one on Cheyenne."

"Huh. Interesting," I said.

That sort of explained why Marc knew about Cheyenne's love life last year. Although I didn't see her advertising her sexcapades for a puff piece in the *Chronicle*. Still, if he'd spent time with her, he would have observed some things. Like maybe even her receiving texts from the mysterious S.O. But that still didn't explain why he had known that Cheyenne had drugged Josh to get him to hook up with her back in September. I filed all this away to consider again later.

"Why are you so interested in Marc and Cheyenne?" Sabine asked, glancing over her shoulder as she held up one of the prints to the wall.

"Oh, no reason," I replied. "He just said something earlier that made me think they knew each other, but I couldn't imagine the two of them hanging out, you know? She'd never have given a guy like him a second glance."

Sabine laughed. "True. She probably would have walked right over him without even noticing." She moved the poster to the small area of wall next to the door and held it up with her arms above her head. "What do we think of this?"

"Looks good to me," I said. I jumped up and grabbed some tape out of my desk drawer. Just as I slammed it, my entire room filled with the sound of Ivy's high-pitched laughter. A cold chill skittered down my spine.

"What was that?" Constance asked, wrinkling her nose.

Sabine's arms dropped along with the poster. "Does Pemberly have an evil ghost?" she joked.

"No, just an evil next-door neighbor," I told them, dropping my voice. "Ivy Slade," I said, tipping my head toward the wall by my bed.

"Ew," Constance said, standing up. "I do *not* like that girl."

"Join the club," I said quietly.

"She's right next door? What bad luck," Sabine sympathized.

I glanced at the wall, the hairs on my neck and arms standing on end. Suddenly I couldn't help wondering whether Ivy could hear what was going on in my room as well as I could hear what was going on in hers.

Maybe it was time for me to start watching what I was saying around here. Just what I needed—to feel even more paranoid in my own room. One more reason to get out of here and back to Billings as quickly as possible. Back to where I belonged.

REPLACED

When I walked out the back door of Pemberly the next morning, my gray cashmere scarf pulled up around my chin, the first thing I saw was a horde of students gathered in the middle of the quad. And at the center of the crowd were Noelle Lange and Amberly Carmichael.

I slowed my steps, not wanting to appear too interested, but dying to know what was going on. As I watched, Amberly tossed her blond hair—which she had clearly straightened this morning—and handed a small white card to Trey. He said something that made her laugh before tucking the card away in his back pocket. Then I noticed that everyone walking away from the circle was clutching one of these cards, and those still in the circle seemed to be clamoring for them. What in the world was going on?

Noelle whispered something to Amberly and they both laughed again, the sound echoing merrily across campus. Watching them made my stomach sink. They looked perfect together, all tucked into their designer coats, puffing clouds of steam into the cold air as they chatted and laughed—like perfectly matched best friends. Surrounded by people, they were clearly the belles of this ball. It was almost like watching Noelle and Ariana from afar last year. They looked that close. That untouchable.

A few weeks ago that had been me. A few weeks ago Noelle and I had been close like that. We had been the center of Easton together. And now . . . now I was merely a loser on the outskirts of Nowheresville. A nothing.

I wondered if Noelle had gotten my e-mail. If she'd read my apology. If I could just get her to talk to me, maybe I could also get her to forgive me for what I had done with Dash. Then she could make the Reed-as-murderer rumor go away. Then I could come back to Billings with a clear conscience and name and everything would go back to normal.

Of course, there was no way to know if she'd read my e-mail unless she decided to come to me. And right now it looked like I was the furthest thing from her mind.

A group of Billings Girls broke off from the crowd and started toward the cafeteria, clutching their cards. Missy and Lorna were among them, but so were Astrid and Sabine. I hesitated for a moment, then realized I could endure the sneers of the former two if it meant I could get info out of the latter pair. I scurried to catch up.

"Hey, guys," I said, falling into step next to Astrid.

Missy scoffed and rolled her eyes.

"Oh . . . hey, Reed," Sabine said tentatively.

"What're those?" I asked, nodding at Astrid's card.

Astrid glanced warily at the others before reluctantly handing over the white square. It was an invitation for a party thrown by Noelle and Amberly. Scheduled for next Saturday evening.

"I don't get it," I said. Why would Noelle and Amberly be throwing a party together? It didn't gel.

"It's a pre-party for Kiran's birthday extravaganza," Astrid said apologetically. "It's so everyone can gather on campus before the party buses come round to get us."

My heart curled into a tight ball inside my chest. I had received my invitation to Kiran's birthday party the week before the fundraiser. The week before the proverbial shit had hit the proverbial fan. But I hadn't thought about the event for days. Other dramas had shoved it to the back of my mind. Did my falling-out with Noelle and my ostracism from Billings mean I would no longer be welcome? Did Kiran even know what had happened? Would she care?

"Everyone's invited. Well, everyone who matters," Missy said snidely, plucking Astrid's invite out of my hand and giving it back to its rightful owner.

I ignored her comment. "Okay, but why Noelle and Amberly? Why are they throwing it together?"

Astrid and Sabine slowed to a stop, as did Missy and Lorna, who hovered a bit behind them. The silence dragged on for so long I was starting to get knee-knocking cold.

"Oh, for God's sake, if you don't want to tell her, I will," Missy said, stepping forward. "It's Noelle's way of welcoming Amberly into Billings. We just voted her in last night."

I felt as if all the stately buildings of Easton had just crumbled around me, shaking the earth beneath my feet.

"Amberly?"

"Yep," Lorna replied. "She's moving her stuff in this afternoon."

I glanced at Sabine, who confirmed it all with one guilty and sad look. Amberly would be moving her stuff into *our* room. Into *my* space. I felt nauseated and dizzy. That was my room. My bed. Mine.

"But she's a . . . a freshman," I stammered.

"So? You were a sophomore when you got in," Missy reminded me. "Clearly if they can bend the rules once they can bend them again."

"Why didn't you warn me?" I asked Sabine, my throat dry.

"I didn't . . . I'm sorry . . . I just didn't want to upset you," Sabine said, as a stiff wind tossed her long dark hair behind her. "After how hopeful we were yesterday . . . I didn't even know we were holding a vote until they woke me up in the middle of the night."

Holding a vote. The Inner Circle ritual. Suddenly I could see it all so vividly. The girls being roused from their beds. The candle- light as they trailed down the stairs in their nightgowns. The chairs in the circle. The marbles being dropped one by one. I could even see Amberly's picture set before them. Her sniveling, smiling little face beaming hopefully out at them.

And they had voted her in. There was no longer an open spot in Billings. I had already been replaced. And by a *freshman*.

"Can we go now? It's freezing out here," Missy said, shoving her hands into her coat pockets.

She and Lorna started for the cafeteria, but Sabine and Astrid hung back.

"I'm really sorry, Reed," Astrid said.

"It's okay," I heard myself croak.

But it wasn't okay. It would never be okay. Because I knew that Noelle had done this on purpose. Just like she'd told everyone about my meeting with Hauer before Thanksgiving and let everyone believe I was a killer. She had chosen Amberly because she had known it would be the ultimate snub. The Billings president replaced by a lowly freshman. She was trying to show me how very little I had meant. How very easy it was to fill my shoes.

She was trying to hammer it home to me that it was over. I would never get back into Billings. Never.

A VISITOR

My Spanish notebook was propped up in front of me, my textbook open to the five-page short story about which I was supposed to write an essay (all in Spanish). I had my English-to-Spanish dictionary out, a new file open on my computer, and iTunes set to shuffle. I was ready to work.

Unfortunately, all I could do was stare at the note I had received from Kiran along with the invitation to her party. I turned the hand-written card over in my hand. Over and over and over.

> *Reed,*
> *It's been TOO long. Please come. Would love to catch up.*
> *x's,*
> *Kiran*

Did the message still apply? Or would she hate me forever once she'd found out what I'd done to Noelle? Was there any possible way she hadn't already heard?

I so wanted to go to the party. I was dying to see Kiran and hoping that maybe Taylor Bell would be there as well. It *had* been too long. But even if Kiran did still want me there, how was I supposed to get to Boston? I could hardly imagine sitting on a party bus with a couple dozen Easton students for the two-hour-plus ride. That long in a confined space with nothing but people who detested me? I'd rather be forced to watch my parents' wedding video nonstop for forty-eight hours, complete with my dad's off-key rendition of Bon Jovi's "I'll Be There for You."

But if I could make it to the party, it might be the perfect opportunity to talk to Noelle. All our old friends together again. Just like old times. Maybe she would find it easier to forgive me if she could be reminded why we'd become friends in the first place.

I sighed and tossed the card down on my scarred desk, gazing at my blank computer screen. There was a lull as iTunes switched songs and I heard a voice, as clear as day, come through the vent under my bed.

"Okay, if you're going to keep doing that, I'm going to have to leave," Josh said with a laugh in his voice. "We're supposed to be studying."

Hot, acidic bile rose up in my throat. What exactly was Ivy doing? About a thousand unsavory possibilities flooded my mind and I instantly reached for my phone. No way was I going to sit in here knowing they were right next door. Not even if I blasted the speakers on both my computer and my CD player. I quickly texted Sabine.

Need 2 get out. Walk?

The few moments it took her to text me back felt like an eternity.

Meet u in quad.

"Thank you, thank you, thank you!" I whispered, grabbing my coat. Sabine was definitely going to win the Best Friend of the Year Award. I turned off iTunes, only to hear a peel of Ivy's laughter that sent my pulse racing. I couldn't get out of there fast enough. I fumbled with the doorknob, trying to pull my coat on at the same time, and tripped into the hall. My door wasn't even closed behind me when I heard another door click shut. I looked up right into the stunning— and stunned—blue eyes of Josh Hollis.

He froze. I froze. He clutched his gray wool jacket in both hands. I stood there half in, half out of my own coat. I guess Ivy had refused to stop doing whatever she was doing to distract him—make me heave— but I couldn't even think about that right then. All I could think about was how he was mere inches from me and how much I wanted to just hug him and how I couldn't.

How I'd never be able to do that again.

I was about to say something—anything to break the awkwardness— but before I could, Josh tipped his head toward my room, silently urging me to let him inside. My heart leapt like a high jumper on speed. He wanted to talk to me. Alone.

I held the door open, my hand trembling, and he slipped past me. The clean, familiar scent of him filled my nostrils and almost made me faint. I closed the door behind us and he turned to me.

"Reed, I—"

I held a finger to my lips. His brow knit, but he shut up. I went over to my computer and cranked up the volume on the Fall Out Boy song my iTunes had last landed on. Then I glimpsed the blue Holiday Dinner card with his name on it and quickly flipped it over before I faced him again.

"I can hear everything Ivy says when there's no music on," I told him quietly—just loud enough to be heard by him. I tossed my coat on my bed. "If you don't want her to know you're in here . . ."

Josh nodded, his mouth set in a grim line. "Got it."

He placed his jacket on the back of my chair and put his battered leather messenger bag down near his feet. His hands went directly into the back pockets of his paint-stained jeans, as if he was afraid of what he might do with them if they weren't secured. Or afraid of what I might do if he kept them within reach.

"So," he said.

"So," I replied, my heart pounding so loud that between it and FOB, I could barely hear.

"How are you?" he asked. "Are you okay?"

His eyes were so full of concern, I wanted to cry. How could he possibly be so nice to me after everything? Yes, he'd already known about the Dash thing before everyone else had—had caught the live show the night of the Legacy before the film adaptation had hit the airwaves. But now that everyone in school had seen it and knew what I had done to him, shouldn't he be hating me with a vengeance? I had humiliated him.

"I'm . . . fine," I lied with a shrug.

It was obvious he didn't believe me, but I was still stuck on the unbelievable fact that he was right there. Right in my room. The two of us. Alone. How many times had I wished for exactly this? How many times had I prayed I would just get one more chance to explain? To win him back? And here I was, a rock the size of a softball in my throat, unable to form a single word in case whatever came out might scare him away.

"I'm really sorry all of this is happening to you," Josh said, running a hand through his curls and looking at the ground. "I know I've been an ass lately, but—"

"Josh, I'm so sorry," I blurted, his words dissolving the softball just like that. "I'm so sorry for everything that happened with Dash. It didn't mean anything, and if I could go back and take it all back, I would do it. You have to know that," I said desperately. "Please, I just . . . I really need you to know that."

I choked on the last few words, and Josh took a step toward me. For a second I thought he was going to take my hand, but then he thought better of it and merely squeezed my upper arm awkwardly before letting his hand drop.

"I know," he said. "I do."

"You do?" I said hopefully.

"Listen, Reed, it's all in the past, okay?" he said, backing off again. "You can't stress about what's already done, especially with everything else that's going on."

Everything else? Didn't he get that he mattered to me more than any of the rest of it?

He picked up my one bottle of perfume from the top of my dresser and toyed with it.

"Just . . . get through finals and everything will be better after break," he said, glancing over at me. "It'll be like a new start or something, you know?" He gestured at my itty-bitty room. "New dorm, new friends . . . You can focus on the SATs and getting into an Ivy and leaving all this behind. Two years from now none of this crap is going to matter anymore."

Except you. You'll still matter.

I felt at that moment that I would be able to leave all of this behind if only I still had him. The person who had always been there for me. The person who had always kept me sane, no matter what was going on around me.

Josh shoved his hands in his back pockets again and faced me. He looked as if he didn't know what to do with himself next. I just wanted him to touch me again. Even if it was another uncomfortable shoulder squeeze. It was so insane, how you could go from kissing and hugging and cuddling someone every single day like it was the most natural thing in the world to not being allowed within two feet of them. It was as if there were this invisible barrier between us and all I wanted to do was breach it. Did he feel even remotely the same way?

I saw his eyes dart past me to his jacket and sensed he was about to bail. But I wasn't ready to let him leave just yet.

"Well, I guess you finally got your wish," I said with a sardonic smile. "I'm no longer in Billings."

Josh's eyes flooded with so much pity I immediately wished I had kept my mouth shut.

"None of this is what I wished for," he said earnestly. "Believe me."

My heart skipped and I looked at the floor, my eyes filling with tears. My computer had clicked over to a slow song, as if it were trying to make the perfect sound track for our conversation.

"Hey," Josh said. He finally reached for my hand, taking it in his. I thought I would never breathe again. "Are you okay?"

I looked up into his eyes, wanting to say about ten million things to him, and that's when we both heard Ivy. The low tones of the slow song were letting her voice come through.

"I can't wait to get Josh to Paris over Christmas," she said, apparently talking into her phone. "Our house on the Left Bank, dinner at Marceau . . . He's not even going to know what hit him."

I dropped Josh's hand and took a step back as Ivy giggled happily. Josh's guilty expression told me everything.

"You're going to Paris with her?" I whispered.

"Not exactly," he whispered back. "My family's going . . . her family's going. . . ."

"I have to get out of here," I said, suddenly feeling as if I was going to overheat. I grabbed my coat and started by him.

"Reed, I'm sorry you just heard that, but—"

I whirled on him, stopping him midsentence. His expression was somehow pleading and defiant all at once. Like he didn't want me to be hurt, but like he also felt I had no right to be hurt.

"Just do me one favor," I whispered to him. "Be careful when it comes to Ivy. There's a lot about her that you don't know."

Then I turned and walked out of my room, leaving my ex all alone inside.

FLOWER BOY

The next day after dinner with Diana and a failed study session in the library, I packed up my notebooks and headed back across the quad toward Pemberly. As I approached Drake House I remembered what Constance had said about Marc doing a story on Cheyenne. And if Marc knew anything about S.O., then I wanted to know too.

Taking a deep breath, I whipped out my cell and dialed Marc's number. His voice mail picked up automatically.

"This is Marcellus Alberro. I'm unavailable right now, but please leave your name and number at the beep and I will get right back to you. If this is about a story, dial pound to page me. Thanks."

"Hey, Marc. It's Reed. I have a quick question for you. Call me back when you get a chance," I said. Then, as I slipped my iPhone back into my bag, I saw a familiar form rushing toward Drake's back door. I hesitated for a moment, knowing I was probably the last person on earth this particular guy would want to talk to, but my adrenaline rush got the better of me.

"James! Hey, James. Wait up!" I called.

The tall, gawky senior turned and looked at me, squinting in the dark. The moment he saw it was me jogging toward him, his jaw clenched. Luckily, however, he didn't sprint off into the night.

"Hey," I said, pausing in front of him. "Do you . . . remember me?" I asked, hoping he somehow didn't. The wind tossed my hair in front of my face and I pulled it away, draping it over my right shoulder.

"The executor of the most embarrassing moment of my life? Sure. How could I forget you?" James replied, shoving his hands into the pockets of his long winter coat.

I looked at the ground, ashamed. Last year Noelle had forced me to break up with James on Kiran's behalf right in the middle of the cafeteria. The whole scene had been so awful I was surprised he hadn't pepper-sprayed me yet.

"Yeah, I'm really *so* sorry about that," I said quickly. "I just have one question for you and then I swear I'm out of here."

James said nothing. He simply stood there, waiting. Something about his steely-eyed gaze made me nervous. Like he was judging me. Which, of course, he had every right to do considering what I had done to him.

"I'm looking for Marc Alberro. Do you know if he's in Drake right now?"

James tipped his head back and laughed, exhaling a cloud of steam into the night air. "Why are you looking for Fourteen-in-Fourteen Flower Boy?"

"Wait. Fourteen-in-Fourteen Flower Boy? That's what we called Trey after he sent Cheyenne fourteen vases of fourteen roses last Valentine's Day," I said, suddenly remembering how Cheyenne's room had smelled like a rose garden for days. "How did you know that? And what does it have to do with Marc?"

James just stared at me. "You didn't know? Trey didn't send her those flowers—Marc did. I figured from the video that all you Billings Girls probably called him Fourteen-in-Fourteen."

Fourteen-in-Fourteen Flower Boy was Marc Alberro? No. Freaking. Way.

"You're kidding," I said aloud.

"Yeah, he was in love with her and wanted to make this grand gesture. I guess it really pissed her off. She humiliated him in front of his entire dorm. I mean, I wasn't in Wesley Hall last year, but I saw the video." James stuck his hands in his pockets and looked embarrassed. "This may sound awful, but at the time it made me feel a little better about what happened to me."

"There was a video?" I asked, still unable to wrap my brain around the idea that Marc had been in love with Cheyenne. I knew he had done a story on her, but how was this possible? How could a guy like Marc even afford all those roses? It just didn't add up.

"Yeah, some guy in Wesley took it with his HDcam. I still have it on my notebook," James said.

"Yeah?" I felt my cheeks redden, but I knew what I had to do. "Do you think . . . I mean, would you mind . . ."

He smiled. "It's okay if you want to see it."

I nodded and followed him back into the dorm. I couldn't believe he was being so solicitous, but I didn't mention it. I didn't want him to change his mind. And there was no way I was going to believe this without visual proof.

James ushered me into the common room off the lobby of Drake House. I hadn't even realized how frozen I was until I entered the saunalike space and felt myself thawing from the inside out. There were a couple of guys in the corner studying, and they shot us curious glances as James whipped out his laptop from his backpack, setting it up on one of the coffee tables.

"Have a seat," he said, gesturing at the plaid couch behind us.

Okay. He was being way too polite considering our history.

"Can I ask you something?" I said as he sat next to me, but at a respectful distance.

"Just did," he joked, reaching for the touch pad on the notebook.

"Seriously, though. Why are you being so nice to me? After what I did—"

"You didn't do that. That was Noelle. I know she made you do it," he said pragmatically.

My skin burned. "Yeah, but I could have said no."

James snorted a laugh and pushed his glasses up on his nose. "No, you couldn't have," he said. "You were new. A sophomore.

From the middle of nowhere. There's no way you could have said no to her."

I checked his expression for any trace of sarcasm or bitterness, but there was none. To him, this was just an accepted fact. Girls under Noelle's thumb didn't have the use of their own free will. Did everyone at this school know that?

"Here it is," James said as a window popped up in the center of the screen.

I leaned in and he hit play and there they were. Marc Alberro, his dark hair slightly longer than it was today, standing in the center of another common room, while Cheyenne read him the riot act. Her hair was longer than shoulder length, as it had been last year, and she seemed shorter than I remembered her. Smaller somehow. She was midsentence when the videographer had started to capture the scene.

"—think this was going to impress me? Fourteen-in-Fourteen?" she shouted shrilly, tossing half a dozen pink and red roses at Marc's feet. She crushed them under the toe of her Louboutin boot. "I've received better presents for *Arbor Day.*"

Marc looked so pale he could have fainted on the spot. Around the room, guys chuckled and nudged one another. At least two dozen of them sat around on the floor, on chairs and on couches, watching Marc's misery unfold. They must have been holding some kind of party, because there were plastic cups and soda bottles everywhere, along with bags of snack food.

"Enough is enough already," Cheyenne said. "I am *not* interested in you. So you can stop texting me, you can stop leaving little presents for me to find all over the place. I already *have* a boyfriend. I don't need a stalker, too."

Marc opened his mouth to say something, but all that came out was a loud squeak.

"Sorry for the interruption," Cheyenne said with a nasty smile, glancing around the room. "You can all get back to your pathetic video game tournament now."

Then she turned and walked out of the room. The videographer zoomed in on Marc's devastated, humiliated face for a split second—the laughter bubbling up in the background—before the feed went black. For a long moment I couldn't even move. My brain was ever so slowly processing everything I had just seen and heard. Stalker? Leaving little presents for her to find? That sounded eerily familiar.

"Guess you Billings Girls are really into the public breakups, huh?" James said wryly, reaching over to close the laptop.

I sat back on the itchy couch, stunned. Sweet, innocent Marc Alberro? Was it possible? And could he really be a cold-blooded killer?

"Yeah," I said finally. "I guess so."

ENEMIES EVERYWHERE

Ivy was at the first sink when I walked into the bathroom that night, still reeling over the discovery about Marc. She was wearing white flannel pajamas and cozy-looking quilted slippers. I was wearing my Penn State sweatshirt and a pair of Easton Academy mesh shorts.

"Got a midnight football game?" she asked with a sneer, reaching for a small pot of some kind of cream.

"Got a midnight facial reconstruction?" I shot back. "Because you could definitely use some softening around the chin and nose."

Ivy's jaw dropped a tad, but she recovered quickly, returning her attention to her beauty ritual with slightly more vigor. I placed my see-through plastic bag of toiletries on the back of the sink and cursed the founders of Billings for giving us private bathrooms. I was so not used to meeting enemies right before bed.

Trying to ignore Ivy, I brushed my teeth vigorously and spat.

Ivy smirked and focused on her reflection, dotting her cream under her eyes and rubbing it in. This was the type of thing that had always fascinated me back in Billings. Did seventeen-year-olds really need under-eye cream? I had asked Kiran once and she had told me it was all about preventive measures. Seemed like a waste of money to me. But then, these people had more money than God.

"What? Fascinated with moisturizer?" Ivy asked, glancing at my reflection in the mirror. She held out the pot of cream to me. "You can have some if you want. Might get rid of some of those insomnia circles you've got going on there," she said, wrinkling her nose. "You do have a lot to lie awake worrying about these days, huh?" she added with mock sympathy.

My face burned and I grabbed my things. "You are such a bitch."

"Oh, please. All that time you spent with Noelle Lange, but *I'm* a bitch?" Ivy said with a scoff, twisting the lime green cap back on the canister. "I can't even hold a candle to her. But one of these days—trust me—that girl is going to get what's coming to her."

My breath caught in my throat as I remembered what she'd said to me on the street that night in New York—how she'd singled out Noelle as the only person left in the Billings ivory tower worth taking down. Hauer had blown me off when I'd told him about it, but now here she was, doing it again—and threatening Noelle even more directly. My fingers clenched and I turned my fiercest glare on Ivy.

"Stay away from Noelle," I warned, speaking through my teeth.

Ivy glanced at me and for the first time looked genuinely interested. "What's that supposed to mean?"

"It means that if you hurt her, or anyone else in Billings, I will personally see to it that you go down," I said, getting right in her face.

Ivy's jaw dropped again, her eyes wide, and she laughed. "You're kidding, right? *Moi?* I'm not the one you should be worried about. I'm not the coldhearted bitch who will step on anyone to get her way. I'm not one who's so addicted to power she'd actually kill someone to take over a dorm."

"I didn't kill Cheyenne," I said firmly.

Ivy laughed again. "Well, duh. I wasn't talking about you."

"Then who were you—"

A cold wave of realization came over me. Ivy was blaming Cheyenne's death on Noelle. She thought Noelle had done it. Or at least she was trying to deflect her own culpability onto Noelle.

"That girl you all worship is capable of a lot of things you could never even imagine, Reed," Ivy said, zipping up her black tote. "Just wait until the truth comes out. Then you'll know. Then you'll finally see her for what she really is."

With that, she swept out of the bathroom, letting the door swing closed behind her.

So this was how she was going to get back at Noelle. How she was going to make the ivory tower fall. She was going to get Noelle to take the blame for *her* crime, while trying to drive me crazy by "haunting" me in the process. Was she punishing me for "worshipping" Noelle?

At least she hadn't succeeded in framing Noelle yet, since the majority of the campus had assigned the guilt to me. I wasn't going to let her get away with it.

I turned and strode back to my room, more determined than ever to prove that Ivy was the real killer. But how? What else could I do? The Internet had long since been exhausted. Of course, I had hours ahead of me to come up with a new plan of attack. After that little encounter it was obviously going to be another sleepless night.

But the moment I walked into my room, I froze. Something was different. Someone had been there. I could sense it. I quickly scanned the room, looking for anything out of place. Then I saw it. The picture of me and Cheyenne from Vienna's birthday party last year—the one Cheyenne's mother had given me to remember Cheyenne by—was tacked to the wall above my bed. My heart started to pound erratically and sweat slicked my palms. How did it get there? Why was it there? Slowly, I placed my toiletry bag down atop my dresser and tiptoed over to the photo, as if it might suddenly attack if I made too much noise.

I gasped when I saw it up close. There we were, Cheyenne and I, smiling broadly with our arms around each other, but you'd never know about the smiles. Because both our faces had been X'd out with black ink.

Trembling, I reached over and snatched the photo off the wall, the tack ripping a hole through the top of it. Hot tears filled my eyes and I tore the photo down the middle. What did it mean? Had someone crossed us out because we were both out of Billings . . . or was the intended message worse than that? Was this just a follow-up to the pills that had been left in my room?

I was about to tear the photo into shreds when I realized it was evidence. Maybe whoever had left this here had left prints. Of course my prints were all over it as well, but still. I fumbled in my bottom drawer for an envelope and dumped the two halves of the photo inside, then stashed it away in my dresser along with all the other "presents" my stalker had left for me over time. The black balls, Cheyenne's pink clothing—it was all there except for the pills and place card, which I had tossed.

Slowly, I sat down on my bed, staring at the contaminated drawer. As my breathing normalized I realized there was no way Ivy could have left that photo in my room. She had already been in the bathroom when I had gotten there and had left about five seconds before me. Not enough time to get into my room, tack up a picture, and get out. Did this mean she was innocent? Was she really not my stalker? Not the killer?

No. I refused to believe it. Until I figured out who S.O. was or found out something majorly disturbing about Astrid or someone else, Ivy was still the only person with a real motive. The only person with a psycho stare. The only person who had both a motive to kill Cheyenne and a motive to stalk me. Maybe she had an accomplice. Maybe she'd gotten Jillian or someone else to put the picture up while I was in the bathroom. Or maybe the photo had been there all afternoon and I just hadn't noticed it.

I quickly opened up my laptop and typed up a new e-mail to Noelle.

Noelle,

I think Ivy killed Cheyenne. You need to be careful. She told me everything about what happened with her grand- mother your junior year. She blames you for everything. Please. If you won't talk to me, at least watch your back.

—Reed

My fingers trembling, I sent the e-mail into the ether, just hoping that Noelle would read it. That maybe there was some tiny soft spot left in her heart that trusted me enough to at least open an e-mail.

Ivy had to be the culprit. She had to be. Because if she wasn't, then I was truly at a loss. And the enemy could be anyone.

NEW QUEEN BITCH

Amberly Carmichael was getting on my last nerve.

As I sat alone at a table in the conservatory on Friday night, she led a group of Billings Girls up to the Coffee Carma counter like she owned the place. Which I suppose she did, technically. But just the counter. Not the entire school. And just to make things worse, the girls she was with—Missy, Lorna, and even Rose, Kiki, and Portia—trailed after her as if she was the new queen bee. As if they were in awe of her. Of a twitty little freshman who would have prostrated herself at their feet a few weeks ago for the mere privilege of talking to them. It was all so very, very wrong.

"Daddy wanted to go to Australia this Christmas. Can you believe it?" Amberly said, loud enough for the entire room to hear. "He has this thing about wanting to surf the Maroubra on Christmas morning and I'm like, '*Daddy!* Get a life!' I mean, I love that he's adventurous and all, but he can surf whenever. He already promised the whole family would go to St. Bart's with the Langes for Christmas, and I was not letting him go back on that one."

"Surfing in Australia? Oh my God, your dad makes my dad sound like a total geriatric loser," Missy said with a snort.

"I wouldn't mind going to Australia with him and watching him surf," Missy added, dropping her Louis Vuitton bag down on the counter. "I saw him when he dropped you off in September, and he's pretty much the hottest dad on earth."

I glanced at Amberly, who looked momentarily grossed-out, as any daughter would be at hearing such a thing, but then she laughed.

"Put your wallet away and order whatever you want," she said, waving a hand at Lorna. "It's on the company. Daddy totally owes me."

I narrowed my eyes at Amberly. She looked different somehow. Softer. Her blond hair was straightened again and tucked back behind her ears instead of overly styled. She wore less makeup than usual, making her look slightly older and more sophisticated. Then there were her clothes. She had unbuttoned her white coat, and underneath were a white turtleneck sweater, skinny jeans, and fringed suede boots with wool peeking out the tops. Her bag was a structured, dark green croc satchel. Looking at the shoes and bag, I realized what had changed. She wasn't as severely matchy as she normally was. She looked as if she had just thrown the outfit together instead of thinking about it for days on end. Which only made her look cooler.

"Thank you *so* much, Amberly!" Missy gushed, double air-kissing the girl as she retrieved her huge coffee.

"Yeah. This is way cool," Kiki added in her signature monotone. She had, of course, gotten a mocha frap with double whip and chocolate shavings. All about the sugar, that one.

Damn. Even realizing that I knew Kiki's coffee preferences made me nostalgic.

Okay, Reed. Get a grip. Back to the task at hand.

Endeavoring to ignore the Billings Girls and how left out I felt, I went back to my list of suspects. I lifted my red pen and finally did what I had been meaning to do all night. I drew a line through Missy and Lorna. When I had Googled them the night before, I had found nothing remotely incriminating or suspect, although I had learned a couple of interesting tidbits. Namely that Lorna had two older sisters, one at Oxford and the other getting an advanced degree from MIT, which might just account for her obvious inferiority complex. And that Missy had had a younger brother who had passed away at the age of eight of leukemia, which made her seem human for the first time ever. But that was it. Nothing else interesting. And when I really thought about it, I realized that neither of them had been acting at all strangely since Cheyenne's death. Missy had ice in her veins, so I could maybe believe that of her, but Lorna . . . Lorna would never have been able to pull off a murder plot without losing it a little. She would have been paranoid, jumpy, weepy, *something*. But she had never been any of the above. It just didn't add up.

Up at the counter, Amberly let out a tinkling laugh and I cringed.

Amazing how the list of people I couldn't stand was growing exponentially, even as my list of suspects dwindled. The only people left on it now were Astrid, Marc Alberro, S.O., and Ivy.

Speak of the devil.... At that moment, Ivy walked through the door, clutching Josh's hand, their heads bent close together as they whispered to each other. The sight of them was a cattle prod to my ass and I immediately stood up to gather my things. There was no way I was going to sit here and watch the two of them get all touchy-feely over lattes. No way in hell.

My sudden movement caught Ivy's attention and she smiled at me triumphantly, reaching up to kiss Josh's cheek as they continued on their way. Josh, luckily, was oblivious to my presence. I wasn't sure if I could deal with the humiliation of him seeing the look on my face right then.

I shoved my notebook into my bag and headed for the door, but my scarf got snagged on an empty chair. I struggled to free it, and when I finally did, I stumbled back a couple of steps. Right into Amberly Carmichael.

There was a sputter and a splash and suddenly my sneakers were covered in light brown liquid.

"Ugh! You bitch! Look what you did!" Amberly blurted.

Her white coat was covered in what appeared to be chai latte, and some had splattered on her white sweater as well. She held the almost empty cup out as the liquid dripped from the hem of her coat to the floor. I pressed my lips together to keep from laughing and glanced over at Rose and Kiki, who along with Missy, Lorna, and Portia were hovering around Amberly. Rose and Kiki both glanced away. Of course.

"Sorry," I said with a shrug.

"You are *so* paying for the dry cleaning," Amberly said, slapping the cup down on a nearby table and grabbing some napkins. "This coat is one-of-a-kind."

She wasn't yelling, just fuming. Fuming and trembling. As I watched her long, pale fingers work at dabbing the stain, I felt this eerie sense of déjà vu, but try as I might, I couldn't place where it was coming from.

"I'm not paying for anything," I told her, shouldering my bag. "It was an accident."

"Oh, you *so* are," Amberly said, glaring at me. Her blue eyes pierced right through me like ice picks. Clearly just a few days in Billings had taught her how to intimidate and awe. "And it's not going to be cheap," she said, looking me up and down with a sneer. "Better start saving your pennies now."

Forget queen bee. Try queen bitch.

Missy, Lorna, and Portia laughed and my skin burned. I even saw a smile playing on Rose's lips for the briefest second and felt as if I had just been stabbed through the gut Caesar-style, betrayed by the people who were supposed to have my back. Kiki was the only one who didn't react, but maybe her iPod was turned up so loud she couldn't hear what was going on.

"Don't hold your breath," I said through my teeth.

"I'll be wanting the Carma Card back," Amberly replied. "And I *will* get my money."

"Yeah. Good luck with that," I said with a scoff.

Then I shot my former friends a scathing look before striding out.

TWO LISTS

I spent Saturday afternoon in the library. Everyone around me was studying. Pencils scratched in notebooks. Whispered debates were being held on everything from the feminist movement of the early 1900s to the history of space travel to the merits of Monet and Manet. At the other computers, coffees were sipped as fingers tapped away crazily at keyboards. I could practically smell the anticipation and tension in the air. Final exams. Final papers. Final oral reports. It was all upon us.

And I was spending my Saturday surfing the Web for a gift for Josh Hollis. Well, that and Googling what was left of my suspect list. I hadn't done one full minute of studying since Sabine had left me an hour ago to go hook up with her bio study group. I was so screwing myself, but I couldn't bring myself to care. I had bigger things on my mind. Like murder. Like first love. Like not letting the murderer—if it *was* Ivy—murder my former best friend.

Sigh.

On the first-love front, it was impossible to find something good for Josh. Nothing said what I wanted it to say. Namely, "I love you. Doesn't this gift remind you of how much you love me?" I had been at it for hours, scouring every shopping site from L.L. Bean to art.com to eBay, but had come up with nothing good. The Holiday Dinner was less than a week away. It was time to admit defeat— especially since I definitely didn't have the money for overnight shipping. I couldn't pay for an Internet gift with what little money I had left from the Billings fund, since it was in the form of cash. All I had was the only-in-emergencies credit card my dad had given me over the summer, and the less I spent on that, the quicker he would be to forgive me. I went back to art.com, selected the Gauguin print I had been halfheartedly eyeing, and just ordered the damn thing.

Sigh, sigh.

The sophomore guy next to me vacated his computer and even before the scent of his raspberry bubble gum had faded into the ether, Marc Alberro had taken his place. He sat down on the chair sideways so that he could face me, the bulk of his winter coat wedged between desk and chair back, his book bag on his lap. Instantly, my heart stopped beating and a tingle of fear shot through me.

"Sorry I haven't returned your message. It's been crazy," he said. "So, what's up?"

I'd been avoiding him since James showed me that video, and glancing over at him now, I found I couldn't even look him in the eye.

Could he be the killer? Had he sneaked into Billings while we were all asleep and force-fed those pills to Cheyenne? Suddenly I felt like I was about to retch.

"What? What's the matter?" Marc asked, tilting his head.

"I have to go."

I grabbed up my things, leaving the RESERVED card on my computer so I wouldn't have to stop to return it to the front desk, and rushed awkwardly for the door. I tried to shove my arms into my coat while semi-sprinting, my bag strap all twisted around my wrist. I attempted to untwist it as I exited the building, but in the process my bag turned upside down, sending all my books and notebooks tumbling down the library stairs.

"Perfect," I said under my breath, crouching to retrieve them. The sky overhead was a threatening gray and wind whistled around the buildings. Any second the clouds were going to open up and pour freezing rain on my head. I could feel it.

"Reed!" Marc was there in a flash. He stooped to help gather my things. "Are you okay? What's wrong?"

As we stood up, our arms full of books, I forced myself to look at him. His brow was creased with concern and his light brown eyes were open and honest. For a second I couldn't imagine that he could have hurt Cheyenne. But after what she had done to him . . .

"You were Fourteen-in-Fourteen Flower Boy!" I blurted, rather more loudly than I intended.

All the color drained from Marc's face. He handed my notebooks to me.

"Well, I prefer to go by Marc," he said, taking a step back and shoving his hands under his sleeves.

My cheeks were flushed with heat. "Marc, this isn't funny. How could you have never mentioned that you and Cheyenne had a thing? Were you hiding it for a reason?"

A group of freshman girls scurried up the stairs between us and I realized it was a good thing this conversation was taking place in such a populated area of campus. If Marc *was* capable of violence, he couldn't get away with hurting me right here, out in the open like this.

"Well, yeah. I had a couple reasons," Marc replied, his eyes wide. "One, it was the most humiliating experience of my life, and two, I don't really relish the idea of getting pounded on by Trey Prescott. Cheyenne *was* his girlfriend last year during the, uh, fourteen-in-fourteen incident. Although I swear I had no idea they were together at the time."

"And that's it. That's the only reason this hasn't come up," I said flatly, thinking of all the times we'd talked about Billings and Cheyenne's death.

Marc stared at me for a moment. "Wait . . . you think I killed her."

"No!" I lied automatically. "No, of course not."

Was there any other way to answer that question? If he had, I didn't want him to know I suspected him. If he hadn't . . . well, same deal. Besides, flat-out accusing him with no evidence to back it up was no better than what everyone was doing to me.

"Yes, you do!" Marc leaned back against the metal bar railing in the center of the stairs. He stared at me for a second longer, then laughed. Laughed. Somehow, that seemed inappropriate given the circumstances. "Well, I guess it would be hypocritical of me to be mad."

"Why's that?" I asked. What was up with this guy?

Marc opened his bag and pulled out a yellow legal pad. He sighed before handing it over to me. Scrawled across the top were the words *Potential Suspects*. My heart skipped a beat.

"You're investigating Cheyenne's murder?" I asked.

"Yeah. I figured it might make a good story," Marc said, his expression apologetic. He shrugged. "I might even be able to sell it to a real paper."

I scanned the list quickly, hungrily, to see if he'd drawn any conclusions different from my own. Unfortunately his list echoed mine. Even Astrid had made his suspect roster. But there were two major differences between Marc's list and mine. My name and Noelle's name were written at the bottom of the page. Noelle's name had been crossed out, but mine had not.

"Sorry. I couldn't play favorites." He grabbed a brown wool hat out of his bag and pulled it low over his ears.

My eyes stung with heat and part of me felt like shoving the pad down his throat. But then I realized he was right. That would have been totally hypocritical, considering I suspected *him*.

"It's fine," I forced myself to say, handing the legal pad back. "Actually, I've been kind of poking around myself."

Marc's eyebrows shot up. "Really? Do you have a list?"

I dug in my bag until I found the folded piece of paper with my suspects on it. Marc looked it over and smirked. "Look at that. You're on mine and I'm on yours. Twice, actually."

I had added Marc's name to the suspect list after seeing James's video, but Marc was now pointing to the initials S.O.

"So *you're* S.O.," I said, stunned.

"Yep." Marc handed the list back to me.

I was at a loss for words. I knew Trey suspected someone by the initials S.O. had been seeing Cheyenne, and I knew that Marc had pursued Cheyenne and lost. How could the two be one and the same?

"I don't get it," I said finally. "Why S.O.?"

"It's a common code when you want to cover up your identity," Marc said with a shrug, pulling a pair of worn leather gloves from his pockets and tugging them on. "Last letter of your first name and last letter of your last name."

S.O. Marcellus Alberro. It was so obvious now I could have screamed. Was all my paranoia and desperation affecting the logical side of my brain?

"Just FYI, I didn't do it," Marc said. "I wasn't even on campus that night. My brother came up from Miami and we went clubbing in New York. He ended up passed out on a bar stool and I had to drag him by his armpits to a cab and take him to the hospital. It was way fun," he added sarcastically. "The cops know all this and have checked it out, by the way."

Apparently the police had been more thorough than I realized.

"Well, I didn't do it either," I told him. "But I have nothing like that for an alibi."

"It's okay. I kind of doubt you'd be investigating her death if you had done it," Marc told me, shoving his legal pad back in his bag. "Wanna go back inside now that you know you're not in mortal peril?" he joked. "It's freezing out here."

"Definitely," I replied, feeling chagrined.

Suddenly I couldn't believe that I had been running from him just moments ago. This whole ordeal was really making me paranoid, and I didn't like the feeling. Marc started walking up the stairs, back toward the library, and I fell into step with him. I took a deep breath of the cold air, letting it whisk away the last of my suspicion.

"I just have one more question," I said. "How the hell did you afford all those roses?"

"Summer job money," Marc said with a grimace. "I thought my mother was going to fly up here just to throttle me when she found out how much I'd taken out of my savings account."

I whistled under my breath as Marc held the door open for me. He must have really liked Cheyenne to risk his mom's wrath like that. Suddenly I hated Cheyenne for the way she had treated him. Why did she always have to make everything such a big, dramatic scene?

"So what have you found out?" Marc asked me.

"You first," I said. "You've decided Noelle is innocent?"

Of course, I already knew this in my heart, but I was curious as to how he had come to the same conclusion.

"Yeah. She was on a boat all night that night. Some charity event on a cruiser that went around Manhattan," he said as he unzipped his coat on our way across the lobby. "There're pictures and everything, so there's no way she did it."

Interesting. I wished Ivy had been around to hear that one.

"Honestly, though? She was my number one suspect until I found that out," Marc whispered, sounding disappointed.

Then, off my offended and baffled look, he continued.

"I mean, after everything that happened last year with Ariana and Thomas Pearson, Noelle just seemed shifty to me. And the fact that she moved right back in after Cheyenne was gone, took over her room, took over your dorm . . ."

"Yeah, yeah. I've heard it all before," I whispered, shaking my head. "God, your best friend goes mentally AWOL and suddenly you're public enemy number one," I joked lamely.

Marc smirked. "So who do you think did it?"

"Ivy Slade," I whispered back.

Marc nodded, unsurprised. "Yeah. She's high on my list too. I know she kind of hated Cheyenne, but I never knew why."

"It's a long story, but for now I'll just say she's got about ten strikes against her. I tried to talk to the police about it, but they won't even listen to me," I whispered.

We dropped our bags at the end of a table in the American history section and the freshman students sitting there stared up at us warily. I stared them down until they blushed and went back to their work. Being a scary murder suspect had its own kind of power. It was less pleasant than Billings power, but it was still something.

"Anyway, Ivy's not about to let me interview her, and the Web hasn't been much help," I told Marc, tilting my head toward the computers. My station was still empty, thanks to the RESERVED sign, but the screen had long since switched over to the Easton screen saver—an Easton Academy crest bouncing around from corner to corner. "But my gut tells me she did it."

"Have you tried LexisNexis?" Marc asked, pulling off his hat and gloves as I shed my coat.

"What's that?" I asked.

He dumped his own coat on a chair and then motioned me to follow him back to my reserved computer. I stood behind Marc as he sat down and brought up a new Explorer page, typing in the address window.

"It's a subscription-only search engine," he said. "I got a username and password at my summer job at the *Miami Herald* and it still works. It's, like, a hundred times more powerful and thorough than Google and pretty much anything else. Plus it only searches reputable publications so you don't get any of that gossip or Facebook crap."

"Sounds good to me," I whispered.

I grabbed an empty chair from a nearby table and brought it up to the desk. Once he accessed LexisNexis, Marc typed in "Ivy Slade" and hit enter. Almost instantly a list of articles appeared. Some of them were familiar—the same articles I had been staring at for days, like the one about the horseback riding competition and Olivia Slade's obit. I was just about to groan in frustration when I noticed a link from the local Village of Easton newspaper—a link I had never seen before. Next to it was a thumbnail photo that, even in miniature, looked mighty familiar. My blood ran cold at the sight of it.

"Open that one," I said, pointing. I felt so jittery that I was amazed at my steady hand.

Marc double clicked. Instantly, the photo filled the screen. Ivy, Cheyenne, Noelle, and Ariana smiled out at us. It was the same photo that hung above Ivy's bed. Marc whistled under his breath.

"That's eerie," he said.

"Seriously."

"'Students from Easton Academy help out with last weekend's Coleman Park Cleanup,'" Marc read, squinting at the caption. "I remember this! It was my freshman year. There was this park in downtown Easton that they wanted to renovate and Easton Academy sent all these kids to help. It was supposed to be a volunteer thing, but everyone who was sent was pretty much being punished for some infraction or another. All of Billings and half of Ketlar went."

"What was the date of the picture?" I asked.

"It was taken on . . . May thirteenth," Marc read.

That freakish tingle of discovery I had been feeling so often lately rushed right through me. May thirteenth. The date was familiar for a reason. That night, Ivy and Cheyenne had broken into Ivy's grandmother's house in Boston and tripped the alarm. That very night Ivy's grandmother had suffered her stroke and Ivy's vendetta against Billings had been born.

This was the picture she chose to keep within sight at almost all times? It had to remind her of the worst day of her life. Why would she keep it so close? Why?

Um, because she's a psycho?

And then, just like that, it hit me. She'd kept it as a constant reminder of why she hated Billings so much. She'd kept it to motivate her in her mission to bring all of us down. Looking at each of the faces in turn, I got chills for a whole new reason.

One committed. Check

One dead. Check.

Noelle was the only one left.

CRYPTIC GIRL

"Well, you've got me convinced," Marc said as we headed out of the library together an hour later. He pulled his hat on and lowered it to his brow line. "I'd say Ivy's a pretty decent suspect."

I had just shared the entire Ivy/Boston/grandmother/Billings story with him and he had been riveted throughout the telling.

"Glad we're on the same page," I replied as I pulled my scarf up to my chin. "But we do still have another person on our list."

"Astrid Chou," we said in unison.

All night I had been wanting to ask him why *he* thought Astrid was a good suspect, but we had been so busy talking about Ivy, I hadn't had the chance. Now he paused at the bottom of the steps, hugging himself against the cold.

"Yeah, she's a weird one," he said as a gust of wind nearly knocked us both off our feet. "Not only do she and Cheyenne have a long history, but no matter what I do, I can't get anyone to tell me why she was expelled from Barton last year."

I yanked my hat on as well and concentrated on not letting my teeth chatter. It was beyond bitter out. "What do you mean, no matter what you do?"

Marc shrugged. "Well, I've tried talking to at least five people over at Barton and they all tell me her records are sealed. Which means that whatever she did, it was really bad."

There was a sinking feeling in my gut and my knees started to shake in the cold. "Define really bad."

"Like, could-be-violent bad," Marc replied, his tone ominous.

My mind immediately flashed back to a couple of awkward moments I had shared with Astrid recently. Her going through my bag at the last soccer game, her bizarre comment about me trying to take Cheyenne's place. And then there were all those arguments she and Cheyenne had had at the beginning of the year. Plus she had been really paranoid when she found out about the Billings disc. . . .

"Damn," I said under my breath as my heart sank even further.

The Billings disc. Why did I have to break that stupid thing? Why had I never made a copy? I would have bet my life that the information we needed about Astrid's expulsion had been in her file.

"What?" Marc asked, visibly shivering.

"Nothing. I'm just an idiot," I told him, starting to walk. If I didn't move soon I was going to turn into a Reed-shaped ice sculpture. "I had this way I could have found out about Astrid, but . . . now I don't."

I had already told enough people about the disc's existence, but at least they had all been in Billings and therefore had a vested interest in said disc. Marc didn't need to know about it.

"Okay, cryptic," Marc said, but he didn't push it any further than that. He walked close to my side, blocking the wind. "What about her friends from Barton? Do you know any of them? Maybe they heard something. I mean, they wouldn't be the most reliable sources, but it could be a start."

A realization hit me and I stopped in my tracks so fast Marc tripped forward in surprise. I didn't know anyone at Barton. But I knew someone who did. Josh Hollis.

"What? What is it?" Marc asked, adjusting his backpack.

I looked west toward the outer buildings. Toward the J.A.M. Building in particular. "I have an idea—someone who might be able to help us," I said, breathless.

"Who?" Marc asked.

"I'll let you know if it pans out," I told him.

Then I turned on my heel and started for the J.A.M. Building. Josh had to be in the studio, working on his final project for his painting class. And if he wasn't, I was just going to have to track him down elsewhere. Right then, he was my only hope.

"Okay, Cryptic Girl! You do that!" Marc shouted after me.

I didn't even bother to turn around and respond. I had to focus. Focus on keeping my nervously beating heart inside my chest. I was going to see Josh. And hopefully I was going to clear my friend. That was about all my brain could handle at that moment.

BOLLOCKS

A fat drop of rain smacked into my cheek about halfway across the quad. Seconds later, the rain was coming down in earnest, and by the time I slipped into J.A.M.'s well-lit hallway, my hair was soaked through and my teeth were chattering. A couple of girls shot me derisive looks as they opened their Coach umbrellas and ducked out into the rain, but I hardly noticed. My mind was racing at the idea of talking to Josh. But I forced myself to keep moving. I walked over to the studio and opened the door.

There were a few students peppered throughout the room, working busily at easels. They all looked up when I entered. Josh was the only one who didn't instantly look away.

"Can I talk to you?" I mouthed to him from the doorway. The place was so silent I didn't want to disturb it any further. Josh dropped his paintbrush and came right over.

"What happened to you? You look like a drowned rat," he said.

"Let's go in the hall," I suggested.

I walked out and dropped my bag on the floor against the far wall of the hallway. Josh leaned back against the opposite one, keeping his distance. Next to him was a large bulletin board papered with information about various clubs and plays and outings. A huge, colorful Holiday Dinner sign was tacked up right in the center, reminding me of how very lame the gift I'd bought him for said dinner was. But that wasn't the point right now.

"Listen," I began. "I know you're going to think I'm insane, and I know you're probably not in the mood to do me any favors—"

"Is this about Ivy?" Josh said grimly, picking at an old piece of Scotch tape on the frame of the bulletin board.

I tried not to cringe. His question was, after all, called for. The last time we'd spoken I'd told him he didn't know his girlfriend the way I did, and then I'd fled.

"No. It's not," I told him. "You still talk to that Cole guy, right? Astrid's ex-boyfriend?"

Josh and Cole Roget had hit it off at Cheyenne's Christmas party the previous year after discovering their mutual love of art, and I knew they had kept in touch via e-mail while Cole was studying in Paris last spring. Josh took a deep breath and stopped picking at the tape, instead tucking his hands behind him against the hallway wall. He looked suddenly uncomfortable. Squirmy.

"Yeah. My brother and I actually met up with him one night in Vienna over the summer. Why?"

I bit my lip and prepared myself for his forthcoming reaction.

Lacing my fingers together, I brought my hands up over my chest and held my breath.

"Is there any possible way you could call him and find out if he knows why Astrid was kicked out of Barton?"

Josh looked at me like I was insane. "What?"

"I swear there's a good reason," I said in a rush. "You know that I wouldn't come here and ask you to do this unless there was a good reason. Especially not after the way we left things."

"No. No way," Josh said, standing up straight and shaking his head. "What would I even say to him? 'Hey, I'm calling you out of nowhere to ask why your ex-girlfriend got expelled?' You're cracked."

I moved away from the hallway wall, hazarding a step toward him. "I know. I know it's insane. But I need to know what happened, and the records are sealed and I think . . ." I looked at him desperately, not sure how he was going to take this. "Trust me. I just . . . need to be sure."

Josh stared at me, looking me over as if he was trying to figure out what to make of me. As if he'd never seen me before. I tried my best to plead with my eyes. Finally, he tipped his head forward, brought the heels of both hands to his forehead, and let out a kind of groan.

"I already know why she got kicked out," he said.

I felt as if the doors at the end of the hall had just burst open and the wind had knocked me sideways.

"You know? How?" I asked, my heart pounding anew.

Josh looked up at me through his lashes. One perfect curl had fallen forward over his forehead. Even with all the intrigue, all I wanted to do right then was kiss him.

"Cole told me over the summer," he admitted, swallowing hard. He crossed his arms over his chest, shoving his hands under his arms and looking off down the hall. Whatever it was Astrid had done, I could tell by his face that it appalled him even to think about it. My throat suddenly went dry. Had Astrid really done something awful?

"What?" I asked, barely audible. "What was it?"

Josh reached back and scratched the back of his neck. His face was turning redder and redder by the second. Whatever he had to say, he really didn't want to say it.

"Josh," I prompted.

"Fine! Astrid slept with her history instructor, okay?" he blurted finally, keeping his voice down so the people in the studio wouldn't hear. "That's why she got kicked out of Barton."

My heart completely stopped beating. Astrid and a professor? I immediately envisioned her making out with the dreaded Mr. Barber—our current history teacher—and almost heaved right there on Josh's boots. But wait. This was good news. Astrid hadn't hurt anyone.

At that moment, the door at the end of the hallway swung closed with a bang and we both looked up to find Astrid herself standing there in a hot pink rain slicker and matching hat, clutching her big black portfolio. It was blatantly clear from the stunned look on her face that she had just heard exactly what Josh had said.

"Oh, bollocks," she said. "How did you find out?"

Josh and I both stood up straight, snagged. Astrid slowly trudged over to us, her black and white polka-dotted rain boots squeaking and squealing on the hardwood floor.

"Actually, it doesn't matter. You're not going to tell Trey, though, are you?" she asked Josh.

Trey? What did she care what Trey thought?

"Don't worry. Your secret's safe with me," Josh said, blushing all over again.

"I'm sorry. What am I missing here?" I said.

Astrid took a deep breath and let it out audibly. She whipped her hat off and tousled her short dark hair before looking at me.

"I've sort of been seeing Trey since the beginning of term," she said.

"What?" I blurted. How did I not know this? Josh and Trey were roommates. How had Astrid and I never talked about this? How had Josh and I never talked about this? Especially back when we were together?

"I know. I know. At first I kept it a secret because I didn't want Cheyenne to find out," Astrid admitted. "I mean, it's like breaking the code, isn't it? You don't date a friend's ex, right?"

Apparently not, if Noelle's reaction to Dash and me was any indication. Josh shuffled his feet uncomfortably.

"Then, after she died, I didn't want all of you to think I was some backstabbing slut, so I just kept my mouth shut," Astrid added.

"That was why you didn't want me to choose Trey off the FYR list!" I blurted. Back when the Billings Girls actually cared about me, they had set up Find Your Rebound to find me an eligible bachelor to help me get over Josh. Noelle had suggested Trey, but Astrid had negged him—supposedly because it would be too weird if I were to date Cheyenne's ex. "Because then you would have had to tell me what was going on."

"The FYR list?" Josh asked.

"Long story," Astrid told him.

I thanked her with my eyes, relieved to avoid having to explain the whole thing.

"But yes, that was why," Astrid said, shaking some water off her hat onto the floor. "And Trey was the reason I was with Mrs. Naylor when we found Cheyenne that morning. I had been out all night at Trey's room playing online games with the blokes and she had just caught me sneaking back in. She was going to bust me, but then we found Cheyenne and . . . I suppose she let it slide."

Astrid looked down at her feet and I glanced over at Josh. The whole thing was just so out of left field, I felt like I needed some kind of confirmation. "Seriously. All three of you were together all night?"

"Yep. Girl's a gamer. She put me to shame," Josh admitted with a smile, reaching over to slap Astrid on the back like she was an old poker buddy

"I can't believe neither of you told me," I said, stunned.

"It's my fault," Astrid said. "I swore Josh to secrecy."

"So, are we done here?" Josh asked, glancing at me. "Because I have a lot of work to do . . ."

My heart twisted painfully. He was so eager to get away from me. First I'd talked crap about his girlfriend and then I'd made him reveal Astrid's dirty little secret. What else could I possibly do to push him further away?

"Yeah. We're done," I told him. "Thanks, Josh."

He gave me the stiffest of smiles before retreating back into the studio.

"I really wish you two crazy kids could work it out," Astrid said, sounding so sincere that it made me want to slaughter myself for ever suspecting her. For ever prying into her private life.

"I know. Me too."

I leaned back against the cool brick wall behind me and let everything I'd just learned sink in, realizing that all of this added up to a major positive. Astrid was innocent. She had been with Josh and Trey all night, and Naylor had discovered her sneaking in *after* Cheyenne was already dead.

As of that moment, there was only one suspect left. And her name was Ivy Slade.

Maybe there was still a chance for us two crazy kids—once I got the third wheel carted off to jail.

BILLINGS JUNKIE

Sunday, I studied in the library. I studied all day long, from 9 a.m. until well after the sun had gone down. Now that I had only one suspect left, I felt somehow more secure. Like I could take a day off. Take a day off and try to salvage my academic future.

It looked like Ivy had decided to dedicate herself to work for the day as well. She had been hunkered down at a table on the other side of the huge bookcase to my right ever since I had arrived. Every half hour or so, I got up to stretch or go to the bathroom just to make sure she was still there. As long as she was studying, she wasn't out somewhere plotting against Noelle, or me, or anyone else. She switched study partners throughout the afternoon, allotting Josh a two-hour stint, which was *so* fun for me, but she almost never left her own chair. Easy girl to stake out.

Finally, it was about two hours after dinner, and I had definitely hit my limit. I had read the same sentence in my history text at least ten times and none of the info had sunk in. It was time to pack it in. But I felt good about my day. I had accomplished a lot. It was quite possible that I could now avoid flunking my finals. A bonus, considering the last thing I needed was to lose my scholarship.

Gathering my things, I stood up and smiled at the other loners who dotted the seats around the table, all hunkered down with their iPods. Not one of them smiled back. Even among the school losers I was persona non grata. But I just let it roll off my back. This had been a good day. I wasn't going to let anyone get to me. After one last check on Ivy's position—still taking notes from her English anthology—I headed for the door.

Outside, I pulled my white wool hat down over my forehead and started carefully along the stone path around the quad. Last night the rain had turned to snow, leaving about three inches of pristine white blanket over the grass. The paths, however, had iced over, and even after a daylong battle by the grounds crews, there were still patches of the slick stuff here and there, just waiting to trip up an unsuspecting student. I kept my eyes trained for any speck of black ice.

It wasn't until I was about ten yards away that I realized I had walked to Billings instead of Pemberly.

I stopped in my tracks, looking up at the tall building that used to be my home, and tears of embarrassment flooded my eyes. How pathetic was I? Pemberly was in the complete opposite direction. Damn my subconscious. Clearly it had a sick sense of humor.

I was about to turn on my heel and rush off before anyone could spot me, when I realized there was music coming from inside. All the lights were on in the foyer and the parlor. Someone on the first floor had cracked a window, and in addition to the music I could hear laughter. Laughter and talking and music.

The Billings Girls were having a party. I saw Portia and Shelby sweep through the foyer, dressed in jewel-toned cocktail dresses and grasping flutes of champagne.

Just walk away, Reed. Don't do this to yourself.

But I couldn't help it. I was drawn to Billings like a junkie in need of a fix. I crunched through the untouched snow, ducked behind a tree, and peeked around the trunk. From there I could see through the huge bay window in the parlor, and the smaller windows in the foyer. And what I saw made me abysmally sad.

They were all there. All the Billings Girls. Everyone dressed to the nines. Fires blazed in both fireplaces and a Christmas tree was decorated in reds and silvers in the corner of the parlor. As I watched, Rose passed out presents from under the tree and a tuxedoed waiter offered a tray of hors d'oeuvres. Everyone looked so happy. So peaceful. So warm. And here I was, staring in from the cold, my shoes filled with rapidly melting snow and tears threatening to turn my lashes into icicles.

Memories of the holiday party Cheyenne had thrown last year flooded my mind. That was the first night I had gotten to know her good side. The first night I had really felt connected to all the Billings Girls, not just Noelle, Ariana, and Kiran. Taylor, of course, had left for home by then. But this used to be my life. This revelry, this decadence, this warmth. It should have still been my life.

Suddenly, two girls stepped in front of the parlor window and sat in the wide window seat, their backs to me. My already cold heart instantly froze over. There was a brunette and a blond. The dark hair and the light. The black dress and the blue. Noelle and Ariana. What was she doing here? Why would they—

No. I closed my eyes and shook my head against the blood rushing through my ears. It couldn't be Ariana. Of course it couldn't.

I opened my eyes again and the girl turned to the side to speak to Noelle. My heart started beating again. It wasn't Ariana after all. It was Amberly Carmichael.

But what was she doing, dressing up as Ariana? Was she *trying* to look like the girl? Because she was succeeding. She was even wearing an aqua scarf—Ariana's signature accessory. Suddenly I realized that this was why that weird déjà vu had hit me the other day in the conservatory when Amberly had frantically attempted to clean her coat of the latte stains. With her softened look, her straightened hair, her slightly boho clothes, Amberly had slowly started to morph into Ariana.

But why? Why would she want to look like a murderer? Did she think that Noelle would somehow like her more if she emulated the girl's former best friend? It made no sense.

Suddenly, Amberly turned toward the window and did a double take. She touched Noelle's arm as if to alert her and I sprang out from behind the tree and ran. I ran straight across the snowy quad, forgoing the icy walkways and cutting my own erratic path through the snow. The last thing I wanted was for Noelle to see me standing out there like some pathetic Oliver Twist–ian waif.

But it wasn't just that. It was also Amberly. Her transformation had me officially freaked. The girl had to be seriously disturbed if she was purposely trying to emulate a cold-blooded killer.

Maybe, just maybe, Ivy wasn't the only person on campus worth looking into after all.

SIDEKICKS

The freshman girls always gathered in the bathroom on the first floor of the class building after fourth period. They would scurry in there in a loud, giggling, gabbing clump and spend at least fifteen minutes doing God knows what before reemerging and heading off to lunch. The rest of us avoided that bathroom like it was the source of a festering boil plague. Honestly, freshman girls could be really annoying. They all dressed alike, they all sounded alike, they all looked alike. I could hardly wait for a few of them to mature, grow their own personalities, and infuse a little variety into the group.

But on Monday after fourth period, I broke the upperclassman rules. I walked downstairs and straight into the freshman bathroom. Instantly all their shrieking and laugher died down. There were at least ten of them in front of the long mirror, fixing their liquid eyeliner and brushing their super-straight hair, but at my entrance, they had all frozen in place like members of some kind of freak, designer-clad mime show.

"I'm looking for Lara and . . . her friend," I said.

Just like that, the entire room emptied out. Bliss compacts were tossed into Cole Haan bags. A dozen pairs of nearly identical Stuart Weitzman booties hurried past me out the door. Only two girls remained, looking like they'd just been cornered by a rabid pit bull. Lara and Nameless. Amberly's two sidekicks. Or former sidekicks. Now that she had ascended to Billings, she was freshman-lackey free. I was hoping to use the fact that she'd kicked the 'kicks to the curb faster than last season's Jimmy Choos to my advantage.

"Hey, there," I said, dropping my bag on the counter next to the white marble sinks. "Don't look so freaked." I looked at the girl whose name I didn't know. She was kind of mousy, with dark blond hair that fell straight down her back. No bangs. No defining features. Her brown eyes were wide as she stared at me, and she was gripping the sink behind her for dear life. "What's your name?"

"Kirsten?" she said timidly.

"Nice name," I said with a smile, trying to get her to relax.

Her lips curled into a small smile. "Thanks. I like yours too."

Lara, who was a bit taller and had slightly darker blond hair that also hung straight down her back, smacked Kirsten's arm with the back of her hand and said something under her breath.

"Listen, I know there are a lot of rumors going around about me, but none of them are true," I told them, crossing my arms over my chest. "And all I really want to know from you is if you remember the night of Cheyenne's . . . death."

I didn't want to use the word *murder*. I had a feeling Kirsten might faint if I did and crack her tiny skull open on the sink. And that, in the words of acronym-happy Portia, would be VNG. The two of them looked at each other for a long moment, then turned to me.

"Yeah . . . ," they said in unison.

"Do you happen to remember what you did that night? And whether or not Amberly was with you?" I asked.

Lara's brow knit, obviously trying to figure out why I was asking. Kirsten, however, jumped right in.

"Oh, yeah. Amberly was totally with us. Amberly's *always* with us," she said, waving a hand.

"Or she used to be," Lara said bitterly. She pushed away from the sinks and took a step toward me, eyeing me discerningly. "What's all this about?"

Okay, so this girl was shrewd. I knew she was on the paper with Constance, so she was probably pulling a Lois Lane here, trying to sniff out my motive and stuff like that. Live the life of an ace reporter as she imagined it.

"I'm helping a friend out with a story," I said, thinking quickly. "You know Marc Alberro, right?"

Lara relaxed. "Marc? Yeah, I know him."

"Well, he's doing an in-depth piece on where various people of interest were that night, so I told him I'd help out with the interviews,"

I said quickly. I glanced at Kirsten and away from Lara's prying eyes.
"So you guys were all together."

"Yeah. That was the night we tried out that new workout DVD,
remember?" Kirsten said, turning as she yanked a lip gloss out of her
bag. She looked at Lara in the mirror. "Some kind of Pilates fusion
thing? Our abs hurt for days. And then, in the middle of the night,
Amberly knocked over that bottle of water we left out and it woke us
all up and you threw your Build-A-Bear at her? Remember?"

"Kirsten!" Lara said through her teeth. She looked at me and
blushed. "I do not have a Build-A-Bear."

I stifled a laugh as Lara's skin tone deepened. "So Amberly knocked
over a water bottle in the middle of the night," I said. "Coming back
from the bathroom, or . . . ?"

"Yep," Lara said, crossing her arms over her chest. "Coming back
from the bathroom."

"No! She went out, remember?" Kirsten said in a scolding tone as
she finished glossing her lips. "She disappeared for, like, hours and
then snuck back into the room at, like, the ass crack of dawn?" she
said, narrowing her eyes as she tried to recall. She lifted a desperate
hand in Lara's direction. "I can't believe you don't remember this.
You were so mad!"

My heart skipped a beat as I took this information in. Disappeared for hours? And Lara was trying to cover it up? Did that mean
that Amberly went somewhere she shouldn't have gone? Did she have
time to—

"It wasn't dawn, Kirsten, it was more like two a.m.," Lara corrected her friend. "I remember that because it was still totally dark out and we had to turn the light on to clean up the spill."

Two a.m. Cheyenne had still been alive at 2 a.m. She hadn't even gotten back to Billings from the headmaster's office until almost one thirty, and then we'd had our fight. And I remember some paramedic saying the estimated time of death was more like 4 a.m. Which would mean Amberly was tucked back in her bed when Cheyenne died. Unless, of course, Lara was wrong—or lying. In any case, where Amberly had gone in the middle of the night was a mystery.

"You're sure it was two a.m.," I said, looking at both of them.

"Positive," Lara said. "Kirsten likes to overexaggerate."

"She's right. I do," Kirsten said with a giggle.

"Well, thanks, girls." I shouldered my bag and tucked my hair behind my ear. "That's all I need to know." I paused before striding out the door. "Say hi to your bear for me," I threw over my shoulder.

I smiled as I walked out the door, even though I'd just proven that bitchy blond upstart innocent. These days, I had to find the fun where I could get it.

Tuesday at lunch I sat with Diana, Shane, and Sonal as they quizzed one another on French vocab words they would need to know for their final. Since I wasn't taking French, I was able to tune them out and stare off into space. Which basically meant I was staring at the Billings table.

Noelle and Amberly sat across from each other at the first seats near the aisle. Noelle in her usual chair, Amberly in my old seat—which was also Ariana's old seat. Her hair was pulled back in a sleek ponytail, and she wore a pressed white shirt under an aqua-colored, cable-knit sweater vest and a gray skirt, plus a light blue scarf. When I squinted, she looked exactly like Ariana. Was I the only person around here who had noticed her transformation? Was I the only one who was totally creeped out by it?

"Have you guys noticed anything different about Amberly lately?" I asked my tablemates, interrupting the vocab round-robin.

"You mean like the fact that she's gone from sniveling bitch to bossy bitch in less than a week?" Shane replied, taking a bite of her ham sandwich. "Has to be a record, even for Easton."

Diana and Shane giggled. Sonal covered her mouth with her hand to keep from spitting her chicken salad everywhere.

"Well, that and . . . isn't she kind of dressing differently?" I asked.

They all leaned in to see the Billings table better. After a moment Diana shrugged. "Still preppy and peppy," she said. "I swear that girl has at least one cable-knit sweater in every color in the universe."

"I thought Seattle girls were supposed to be more, like, earthy," Sonal commented, tossing her long black hair behind her shoulder as she sucked at her teeth.

"Apparently Amberly didn't get the memo," Shane replied.

"But she doesn't look like she's trying to emulate anyone else?" I prodded.

They glanced over again. "Laura Bush?" Shane suggested.

Then they all cracked up laughing and got back to their work. So much for that. Maybe it was just because I had known Ariana better than they had. Or maybe I was just trying to see something that wasn't there. And there was always the chance that I was getting a tad obsessed with this whole Cheyenne murder thing.

I was about to return to my lunch when Kiran's ex—Dreck Boy James—walked by Noelle with his tray of food. She said something to him as he passed—something I couldn't hear, but which cracked up the other girls at the table. James paused for a moment, turning beet red. For a second I thought he was going to say something back, and I willed him to do it. To just stand up for himself. But instead he ducked his head and kept walking.

Noelle smiled happily to herself as she sipped her water, and suddenly all those feelings from that awful day last year came flooding back. The terrified look on Kiran's face when Noelle had told her they knew who she was dating. How Noelle had basically blackmailed her into breaking up with James. How atrocious and nauseated I had felt when I had been the one forced to do it. As much as I had grown to love Noelle, I wished that just once she could get a taste of how she made other people feel. Just once I wished someone would blackmail *her* or make *her* feel less than worthy.

At that moment I so wished I hadn't destroyed that Billings disc. It would have been such perfect blackmail material. If I still had it, I could use it to get her to listen to me. Get her to finally hear my side. Maybe even get myself back into Billings. Damn my temper. Why did I have to go and crack the thing in half without thinking ahead to—

And then, just like that, an intense wave of heat overcame me. Just like that, epiphany. I could have made a copy of the disc. I hadn't, of course, but I *could* have. All I had to do was make Noelle believe that I still had the information and the upper hand was mine. For the first time since she had booted me from Billings, I felt an exhilarating thrill of possibility. For the first time I could taste my comeback.

I knew I would have to put my Noelle plan into action ASAP, before I lost my nerve. The only problem was, the girl never went anywhere alone. If I had any shot of getting her to listen to me, she was going to have to be solo, because when other people were around she wouldn't be able to give me an inch. That would be perceived as a weakness, and she couldn't have that.

So that night I called Sabine and asked her to keep an eye on Noelle for me. If the girl did happen to leave Billings on her own for any reason, Sabine was to call me. Much to my surprise, Sabine didn't even ask me why I needed this info. She probably just assumed I was going to try to beg my way back into Billings. Right end game, wrong method.

The call came in the next morning. Early. My heart was in my throat as I fumbled to answer my phone, unaccustomed to sudden blasts of music at such an ungodly hour.

"Hello?" I said, breathless, trying to shake the sleep from my head.

"Noelle and Amberly just left for Coffee Carma. They're meeting up with their party planner to visualize decorations for the pre-Kiran thing before Coffee Carma gets crowded," Sabine whispered to me. "I know she's not alone, but it's close. It might be your only chance."

"Thanks, Sabine," I said, tossing the covers aside.

"Good luck," she replied just before I turned off the phone.

I dressed quickly, throwing on a black turtleneck sweater and pulling my hair back into a ponytail. In the bathroom I threw some cold water on my face and looked at my reflection. I looked tired and pasty, but I was just going to have to make the best of it. I grabbed my Chloé bag and my books and raced from the dorm.

The campus was cold, gray, and mostly deserted, the once pristine snow now decimated by a thousand muddy footprints. I passed by Mr. Cross on his morning stroll and slipped into Mitchell Hall. My heart bounced around in my chest as I approached the conservatory and I took a deep breath, endeavoring to compose myself. Noelle could not see me looking anxious or tentative. I had to appear in control. Confident.

"I'm thinking color. Lots of garish, over-the-top color," Noelle was saying as I entered the room. Her voice echoed in the high-ceilinged space as Amberly and the party planner followed her along the window wall. She wore a black knit dress, black tights, and black boots, while Amberly wore a very similar outfit, but in white. With the blue scarf, of course. "I'm sick of white twinkle lights. Enough already. Let's get hot pink and red and purple. Let's make it a sultry, glam Christmas thing."

"Brilliant," the party planner said, making a note on her clipboard. She was a tall, lithe woman with shorn red hair and tiny square glasses. Her kelly-green wide-leg pants were beyond trendy, and they made her waist look like it had the same circumference as a soda can. "Simply brilliant."

"Everyone's just going to *die*," Amberly gushed.

Noelle shot her a brief look of scorn, and I knew exactly what she was thinking—*so* gauche. Hadn't someone already died? So apparently, Amberly wasn't totally perfect in Noelle's eyes. The thought awoke a warm, fuzzy feeling in my chest.

At the Coffee Carma counter someone fired up the foam maker and the noise caught the threesome's attention. They all turned and spotted me hovering.

"Oh, look," Noelle said, looking down her nose at me. "It's my stalker."

The party planner's eyes widened in alarm. Her trembling hand went right to the oversize beaded necklace at her throat. Clearly Easton's reputation as the murder capital of the private school world had gotten around. And I guess I did look a little wild-eyed, considering what I was about to do.

"Seriously, Reed. It's getting a tad pathetic," Amberly added with a sniff. "And if you're looking for an invite, keep looking."

Noelle and Amberly both laughed and turned back to the window. The party planner followed suit, pointing out the challenges of the floor-to-ceiling windows and listing a few ideas of how to deal with them.

"Noelle, enough is enough. I need to talk to you," I said, my voice strong and clear as a bell in the wide room. "It's a matter of life and death."

Noelle *tsk*ed and slung her thick hair over her shoulder. "So dramatic."

That was it. I walked right over to her, grabbed her arm, and forcibly pulled her away from the others.

"What are you doing?" Amberly blurted.

Noelle actually tripped sideways, taken off guard by the physical attack. But the moment she composed herself she pulled away, smoothing the front of her knee-length dress.

"You did not just touch me," she said.

"I'm sorry, but I had to get your attention," I told her under my breath. "Have you even read any of my e-mails?"

Amberly had almost reached us, but Noelle held up a hand, stopping her in her tracks. The girl looked confused for a moment, unsure of what to do, before she sullenly returned to the party planner.

"Uh, no," Noelle replied. "Those little missives have been directed straight to the recycle bin."

I pressed my lips together, frustrated. "You shouldn't have done that. I—"

"Miss Lange? Everything all right over there?" the party planner asked.

"Fine," Noelle replied, lifting a hand. "This won't take long. Why don't you two talk Christmas trees? I'm thinking faux, faux, faux. Maybe something in feathers." She looked at me again, her brown eyes bored. "Go ahead. What could possibly be so very important?"

"I think Ivy killed Cheyenne," I told her, my pulse quickening. "In fact, I'm about ninety-nine percent sure she did it. And I think she's going to come after you next."

Or me, I thought, dread radiating through my stomach as I recalled the pills and the defaced photo of myself and Cheyenne. But there was no reason to bring my own peril into this conversation. In order for me to keep Noelle's attention, this had to be about Noelle.

Unfortunately, all she did was let out an incredulous laugh that filled the room. "Ivy Slade? That girl does not have the balls. Nice try, Glass-Licker, but no sale."

She started to turn away from me. Classic Noelle egotism. Didn't she get that she was in danger?

"Okay. Let me rephrase," I said, putting on my best condescending tone—one I had learned from Noelle herself. One I knew she would respond to. "What if I told you she's still pissed about how you, Cheyenne, and Ariana left her alone at her grandmother's her sophomore year?"

Noelle whipped around to face me again. I'd never seen her react so automatically, so fiercely. Normally she took a moment to pause, consider, and collect herself before reacting to anything.

"What do you know about that?" she asked, going pale.

I allowed myself a moment of triumph. Finally I'd done it. I'd actually gotten her to feel that paranoid uncertainty that she made others feel every single day. She didn't appear to enjoy it any more than the rest of us did. And I wasn't even close to finished.

"I know everything," I said, lowering my voice and taking a step closer. "Including the fact that Ivy blames you, Ariana, and Cheyenne for her grandmother's stroke—and death."

Noelle blinked, her eyes filling with something that looked a lot like fear. I was getting to her. She was finally, finally listening to me.

"Don't you think it's all a little suspect?" I asked. "Ivy comes back to school this year and Cheyenne ends up murdered within a month? Ariana's in an institution, so she can't get to her, but you . . . you're right here. You're next."

"Why are you doing this?" Noelle asked, her voice strong but her eyes uncertain. "Why are you trying to scare me?"

"I'm not," I told her. "I'm trying to warn you. I'm *trying* to protect you."

Noelle looked me in the eye and for a split second, I could see her start to cave. Start to realize that I was still her friend. That we needed each other. That one stupid night with one stupid guy should not get in the way of all that. But then, out of nowhere, her face turned to stone.

"And don't tell me. You feel you need to be living in Billings to properly protect me, right?" She let out a short, incredulous laugh.

"You're really grasping at straws here, Reed. And desperation, by the way, is not becoming."

"Noelle—"

"I don't need your protection, Glass-Licker. I don't need *anything* from you," she said, crossing her arms over her chest. "You know what I think? I think you must have way too much time on your hands over at Pemberly if you're making up stories like this. *Way* too much time."

Her smile was mocking. She knew I had been watching her through the window on Sunday night. She knew just how pathetic and lonely I was.

"I'm not making this up," I said, needing her to understand. "I'm worried about you."

"Well, thanks for the tip," she replied blithely. "I'll make sure to keep an eye out for a wannabe loser wielding pills."

She turned to go again and I knew what I had to do. I didn't want to, but I had to. It was blackmail time.

"You're wrong," I said to her. "You do need me."

Her shoulders slumped dramatically as she turned to me once more. "Oh, really? And why's that? Are you going to teach me all about the ins and outs of NASCAR?"

"A dig at my Middle America upbringing. How original," I said sarcastically. I pulled the Chloé bag out from behind my book bag and dropped it on one of the small Coffee Carma tables. "Remember the disc that came with this?"

Noelle hesitated. This time I knew I had her. She had not been expecting this.

"Yes," she said slowly. "I believe you destroyed it right in front of my face."

I stared straight into her eyes and just prayed she wouldn't be able to tell that what I was about to say was a complete lie.

"I made a copy. How stupid do you think I am?" I said.

Inside I knew exactly how stupid I was, but she didn't need to know that. She studied my face, and I made sure not to blink.

"I still have it, Noelle," I said. "I can zap that information to the entire school, to the entire Easton community—alumni and parents included—at any time. Everything there is to know about you and all my Billings sisters. Out there for all the world to read and enjoy."

Noelle's expression was baffled, incredulous. I had her. I so, so had her.

"Are you trying to blackmail me?" she said merrily. "That is *so* cute!"

Okay. So maybe I didn't have her.

Her dig got right under my skin. I was losing control of this thing. Losing big time. But I wasn't about to give up just yet.

"Let me back in Billings, Noelle," I said under my breath. "Let me back in or I'll do it. I'll e-mail all the files to everyone we know."

Noelle narrowed her brown eyes. "Go ahead," she said. "There's nothing on there that I'm ashamed of. And as for the others, if they have skeletons, that's their problem. Go ahead and send it. The aftermath might actually be fun."

"So you're saying you'd rather have all your housemates and friends humiliated—in some cases devastated—than let me back in," I said, disbelieving.

Noelle smiled ever so slowly, causing my heart to drop to my toes.

"Yes, Reed. That is exactly what I'm saying."

MINI ARIANA

I was getting nowhere. With Noelle, with Josh, with my schoolwork. That night I sat at a table on the first floor of the library, staring straight ahead at the spines of the books on the opposite shelf. Didn't even try to pretend I was studying. There was no way I could concentrate.

Noelle was never going to let me back into Billings. Josh was never going to let me back into his life. And no one other than Marc would believe what I knew to be true about Ivy. I might as well just flunk out of school. What could possibly be the point of staying here anyway?

"Hi, Reed."

Sabine slipped into the chair across from mine and glanced at my textbook. "English? Good. I'm so behind in English. Want to work together?"

I looked at her eager face, her hair pulled back in a thick French braid, and sighed. "Sure. But I need to refuel. I'm just going to go get some chocolate." I grabbed my wallet from my bag and stood up. "You want anything?"

"No, thanks," Sabine said cheerily. So cheerily I was starting to wonder if she thought she could raise my mood by osmosis. So far, not working. But I applauded her effort.

I walked along the wall to the little alcove where the vending machines were housed and waited while a pock-faced boy selected his candy bar of choice. When he turned and saw me, he started visibly then slid away from me like I was on fire. I shook my head and started to feed my coins into the machine. People really were just so juvenile.

"Hello, Glass-Licker."

Amberly Carmichael strode into the alcove and leaned one shoulder up against the vending machine, so close I could smell the minty freshness of her breath. She wore a pristine white sweater coat with a faux fur collar and that aqua blue scarf around her neck. Her blue eyes narrowed as she stared me down. Even up close, her resemblance to Ariana was enough to chill my bones.

"You don't get to call me that," I said through my teeth.

"Actually, I think I can call you whatever I want," she said. "You've become that insignificant. It would be sad, really, if you didn't deserve it."

I simply stared at her. I was so stunned by her audacity, I couldn't even begin to address it.

"Listen, Reed." She said my name as if its four letters polluted her mouth. "I heard everything you said to Noelle this morning. You should really work on your blackmail voice," she said, lowering her own voice to a near whisper. "I know about the disc. And if you think for one second that I am going to let you make any of that information public, you are sorely mistaken."

Laughter bubbled from my lips. "Oh, am I?"

A cold, angry look flashed across Amberly's face and my heart halted. Ariana. So Ariana. "I would do anything to protect my Billings sisters."

Even as my mind drew the disturbing comparisons between this nut job and the other, I had to laugh again. I couldn't help it. Whatever airs she was trying to put on, whoever she was trying to morph into, this little upstart had been in Billings for a few days. I had been there for over a year. Those girls were more my sisters than they would ever be hers.

"I'm glad you think this is so hilarious," Amberly said, putting her hands behind her back. "But I want that disc, and if you don't get it to me by tomorrow evening, you are going to be *very* sorry."

I could just imagine what amounted to consequences in Amberly's world. "What're you going to do? Throw a Build-A-Bear at my head like your little friend did to you?"

For a split second the old, wide-eyed Amberly was back. Clearly she was caught off guard by my insight into her personal life. Noelle would have been so proud of me. If she'd been at all inclined to feel for me anymore.

"Gee, Amberly, thanks for the warning," I said, seizing my moment. "I'll be sure to keep an eye out for flying stuffed animals."

I started to walk away, feeling rather good about myself, but her hand shot out and grasped my arm.

"The bill," she said, holding a yellow slip of paper up in front of my face. "For the dry cleaning."

Bitch. Bitch, bitch, bitch.

"You can give me the money tomorrow when you give me the disc," she said with a smirk.

She sidled out of the alcove just as Sabine walked in. Sabine looked at me, clearly sensing the thick tension in the air.

"Hi, Sabine," Amberly said brightly as she passed her roommate by.

"Hi," Sabine replied hesitantly. "What was that about?" she asked me the moment Amberly was gone. She glanced at the dry-cleaning slip in my hand.

"Her bill," I said, holding it up. "For the dry cleaning."

The thin paper trembled in my hand. I was bubbling with anger.

"No. I thought she was kidding," Sabine said, incredulous. "You're not going to pay it, are you?"

"Um, no," I replied, crumpling the receipt and shoving it into the pocket of my jeans. "I really don't like that girl."

"Join the club," Sabine said, slipping by me to feed some cash into the candy machine. "I decided I needed some chocolate after all. What do you want?"

"Nothing, thanks," I said, taking a deep breath. "I'm good."

Chocolate was no longer needed. The adrenaline rush should keep me going for at least an hour. And if I never saw mini Ariana again, it would be way too soon.

DÉJÀ VOMIT

I trudged back to my room later that night, my body weary, my eyes at half-mast. I had stayed at the library far longer than I had intended, and I could still feel the hard, uncomfortable library chair pressing into the small of my back. My brain hurt from the number of literary characters and motives and plots Sabine and I had re-crammed in there, and my fingers had atrophied from taking notes. The good news was, I was so tired, I would probably pass out in about five minutes. There would be no lying awake staring at the ceiling and letting the cold, suffocating blanket of loneliness overcome me. No obsessing about my tiny single and everything it represented. No fretting about pills and X'd-out photos and other morbid gifties.

But then, in the dimly lit, carpeted Pemberly hallway, about five steps away from my room, a familiar scent tingled my nostrils. I froze. My heart seized with fear and I tried to breathe through my mouth, but it was no good. The smell was so strong I could taste it.

Cheyenne's perfume. The sickly sweet floral scent of Fleur. It filled my senses. Someone had sprayed it all over the hall.

No. No, not again. Not again. Of all the presents my stalker had left me, this was always the most haunting, the most visceral, the most . . . Cheyenne.

I stared at the closed door of my room. Someone on the floor was listening to Bach at top volume. My head started to pound along with the racing tempo.

Run. Just run. Don't go in there. Nothing good can come of going in there.

But where else did I have to go?

Trembling from head to foot, I stepped over to my door. Placed my hand around the cold doorknob. I closed my eyes and said a quick prayer. That I was just imagining things. That my room would be exactly as I had left it. And then I pushed the door open and flipped the light on in one quick motion.

One look at what lay before me and I staggered backward. My vision blurred and I had to brace my hands on my knees to keep from buckling over.

"No." The word escaped my lips. "No, no, no."

Somewhere on the floor a door slammed. Startled, I clung to the cold metal of the doorjamb and pressed my hot face against it, my eyes wildly scanning my room. Why was this happening to me? Why?

My bed had been stripped, the comforter balled up on the floor, the pillows uncased and tossed at the foot of the bed. The sheets trailed across the floor. Crushed into the throw rug in the center of the room—the brand-new, cheery throw rug Sabine had given me—were dozens and dozens of blush beads. Pink and brown powder everywhere.

I started to hyperventilate, breathing in the scent of Cheyenne's perfume until it started to poison my brain. Cheyenne. She had done this to me that first day of chores last year. That day I had been woken from my bed in Billings and forced to do whatever the residents asked of me. Cheyenne had told me she liked her pillows fluffed, her sheets tight. And when I had talked back to her, she had crushed an entire pot of blush beads into her white and green flowered rug. She'd demanded I clean it up.

Suddenly, my dinner decided to make a reappearance. I turned away from my room and fled for the bathroom. I dropped my book bag in the hallway and clawed off my coat. My knees hit the hard tile in the first stall just in time. Everything I had eaten in the past five hours came right back up. Tears streamed from my eyes as I retched. Luckily the bathroom was empty. Thank goodness for small favors.

Finally, I sat back on my butt and flushed the toilet. I wiped my hand across my mouth and nose and dried my tears, shaking uncontrollably. My temples were pounding, my vision blurred.

My stalker had sunk to a new low. That had been one of the worst mornings of my life, and my first real introduction to Cheyenne. Seeing those blush beads brought her back to me more vividly than any of the other pranks and plants I had endured—even more than the perfume. Whoever was doing this really was trying to drive me crazy.

And maybe they were succeeding. A girl could only take so much.

I pressed my palms into the cool tile at my sides and pushed myself up. I cleared my throat as I stepped tentatively from the stall and around the partial wall that separated the toilets from the sinks and showers. There I found out I was not, in fact, alone. Ivy stood at one of the sinks, smiling happily at me.

"Okay, *that* was disgusting," she said to me, shouldering her bag. "Bulimia is *so* last century, Reed. Next time you want to toss your cookies, do it in the privacy of your own room. That's what plastic trash cans are for."

Then she turned and sailed out of the room, her nose in the air. I stared at myself in the mirror above the sink, my eyes rimmed in red, my nose all puffed up. And just like that I felt another wave of nausea. Because Ivy could not have pulled off this particular prank. She hadn't even been here last year. There was no way she could have known about my first chore day. No way she could have known what Cheyenne had done to me. I gripped the sides of the sink and stared into my own terrified eyes.

All this time I had been so sure that it was Ivy. But the only people who knew about what had happened that morning were Billings Girls.

THE ENEMY

After scrubbing the rug in the sink, remaking the bed, and cracking open my window to clear the smell (which took all my strength and about twenty minutes of struggling against years of paint buildup), I finally crawled into bed. Then I lay there wide awake, shivering against the cold streaming through the screen, petrified to close my eyes.

If not Ivy, then who? If not Ivy, then *who*? Who would want to torture me like this? I had plenty of enemies now, sure, but when all of this had started, there'd been no one. No one but Ivy, who hated everyone in Billings. Or Ariana, of course, but she was locked up somewhere. If it wasn't Ivy, then I was at a loss. If it wasn't her, then it could be anyone.

If only I could talk to Noelle. She would know what to do. She would know exactly how to sniff out my stalker, how to catch the person in the act or smoke them out or *something*. At the very least she could talk me down. Make me feel better about the situation. Make me feel above it all. Make me feel safe.

But that was never going to happen. Noelle was never going to forgive me. I was on my own.

As I stared at the swirls in the crumbly stucco ceiling, a thousand thoughts whirled in my head, but one kept squirming its way to the forefront.

I had to win Noelle back. She was the key to putting an end to all of this. She was the key to winning back my life. I wished I had told her about the stalking from the beginning, but I had been too proud. Too afraid to let her know there was a chink in my armor. And look where that attitude had gotten me.

I should have been in my comfy bed in Billings right then, snoozing my cares away. I should have been the one throwing parties with Noelle and shopping for extravagant gifts and planning my Christmas vacation to St. Bart's.

Instead I was lying in my tiny room all alone, with Josh's lame-ass Christmas gift leaning up against the far wall, listening to Ivy as she giggled on the phone, while I was stuck looking forward to yet another gray holiday in dreary Croton, Pennsylvania. And, oh, yeah, I was potentially living next door to a killer. The same girl who was, right now, flirting with the love of my life right on the other side of this crappy wall. The same girl who was potentially plotting my former best friend's murder.

At least as long as she was in there flirting, she wasn't out there killing anybody. I supposed there was always a bright side.

I rolled over onto my side and groaned, balling the sheet up in my hand. How could I get Noelle's attention? How could I get her to take me seriously again? How could I make it all up to her? Everything hinged on that. If I could only get back in with Noelle, I could not only have *my* life back, but I could protect—even save—hers.

I had to do something. But what? How could I show Noelle how much she meant to me? Thanks to me and my seven minutes in heaven with Dash, she had been publicly humiliated. How did a person make up for that?

Suddenly, I sat up straight in bed, so excited I almost choked on my own breath. The answer was so obvious, so blatantly obvious, I couldn't believe I hadn't thought of it before.

I threw my covers aside and jumped out of bed to power up my computer. I finally had a plan. And this was going to work. It had to.

ROSE AND IVY

Thursday morning I was exhausted and foggy and out of it. Even after my Noelle epiphany, I hadn't been able to do anything but obsess all night long. I couldn't even fathom making small talk, so at breakfast I decided to sit alone. I dragged my butt over to one of the smaller tables near the wall of the cafeteria and dropped into a cold chair. Supporting my head on my hand, I poked at my Cheerios, shoving them down into the milk until each one was so soggy I didn't want to eat it at all. My eyes hurt. The skin around my eyes hurt. Even my scalp hurt. I had never been so tired, so frustrated, so scared in my life.

All I could do was hope that my plan for Noelle would work. All I could do was hope that the stalker wouldn't attack again before I won her back. Because I wasn't sure how much more of this I could take.

What would I do if it didn't work? Who would I turn to then?

A familiar laugh caught my attention and I looked over at the Billings table. There was Noelle, her head thrown back in laughter, looking fresh-faced and gorgeous and carefree. Didn't she see how miserable I was? Didn't she care at all?

Then Sabine stepped up to my table, blocking my view.

"Hey," she said tentatively. "Do you mind if I sit?"

"You probably shouldn't," I told her flatly. "Noelle will make your life a living hell."

"I don't care."

Sabine set her tray down and smoothed her brown tweed pencil skirt underneath her as she sat. She slid her linen napkin out and unfolded it on her lap.

"You're my friend, and if Noelle doesn't like it, *c'est la vie*," she said.

I was so touched, my eyes filled with tears. Sabine was the only real friend I had left. Even Constance only spoke to me when there was no chance of her being caught. Not that I didn't understand. Constance was, after all, terrified of Noelle. As I had been last year. But that just made Sabine's sacrifice all the more special. Now I needed both hands to hold my head up.

"Reed? What is it? Are you all right?" Sabine asked, concerned.

"No. I'm not," I said, staring down at my cereal bowl. My voice was thick with unshed tears. "It's happening again."

One hot tear escaped the corner of my eye and I let it run right down the side of my nose and plop onto my tray. I was so tired. So, so, so tired.

"What?" Sabine asked, breathless. She leaned into the table. "What's happening again? Reed, you're scaring me."

Don't do it. Don't tell. You've kept the secret so long—why tell now?

Because I'm exhausted. Because I need help. Because everyone already thinks I'm crazy anyway.

I looked up at Sabine. Her green eyes were wide with worry. She was clearly the only person who cared about me around here. The very thought was so overwhelming, I caved like a paper tent.

"Someone's stalking me," I whispered, my face hot with shame.

"What?" Sabine gasped under her breath. She balled her napkin up in her hands and twisted. "What do you mean?"

"For the past couple of months, someone has been leaving things for me to find . . . things related to Cheyenne," I said in a rush. I couldn't believe I was finally letting this out, but it actually felt kind of good to share it with someone—freeing. "They were in our room. They left black balls in my drawer and Cheyenne's clothes in my closet, and they planted that perfume in my bag the day of the fund-raiser, and they sent me these e-mails as if they were from Cheyenne. Hundreds and hundreds of e-mails. I think they even fished that photo of me and Cheyenne out of my bottom drawer and pinned it to my bulletin board that time . . . remember?"

Sabine bit her lip. "Which picture?"

I was so frustrated I dropped both hands on the table, which caused a clatter of silverware and dishes. "Forget it. It's not important. But whoever it is has gotten really crazy since I moved into Pemberly." I looked around to make sure no one was in hearing distance, then lowered my voice just to be sure. "They left me those pills. The same ones Cheyenne used to kill herself. Or, well, I mean, the same ones the murderer used to kill her, I guess."

Sabine gasped and covered her mouth with her hand. "What?"

"Yeah. And that photo of me and Cheyenne, well, they pulled it out again, but this time they X'd out the faces. And last night they destroyed my room. Left the bed unmade and did this other stuff that Cheyenne once did to me. . . ." I stopped, gasping for air. Someone at a nearby table laughed, and a glass broke on the other side of the room, drawing a quick round of applause—reminding me of where I was. For a moment I think I'd been so focused on my story, I'd forgotten. "Sabine, I don't even want to go back to my room."

For a long moment Sabine said nothing. She sat back in her chair, rock still, and stared down at the table, clearly trying to process everything I'd said.

"I can't believe this," she said finally. "Why did you not tell me this before? This person sounds dangerous."

"I didn't want you to think I was crazy," I admitted, toying with my water glass. "I thought I could handle it on my own. Or I thought it would go away. But it hasn't. It's only gotten worse."

Sabine pushed her tray forward and folded her arms in front of it. "And you have no idea who it is?"

"No," I said miserably. "I thought I did, but . . ."

Sabine folded her napkin back over her lap. She pushed a stray strand of dark hair behind her ear and looked straight at me.

"This may sound weird," Sabine said tentatively. "But have you considered Ivy?"

I had felt as if I had been spinning and spinning and spinning in place and someone had just held out a hand to stop me. As if the whole world had just snapped back into focus. Finally.

"Why? Do you know something?" I asked.

Sabine glanced over her shoulder before leaning in even farther. "I didn't think anything of it at the time, but I saw Ivy inside Billings the morning of the fund-raiser."

All the hairs on the back of my neck stood on end. "Inside? How?"

"I think . . . I think she was visiting Rose. At least, she was coming out of Rose's room," Sabine admitted. "I figured they were old friends so it didn't seem that strange to me, but now . . . it's kind of a big coincidence, no? She could have left Cheyenne's perfume for you that day."

My mind reeled and a cold shudder passed through me, making me cling to my cardigan sweater. Rose. Could Rose have been letting Ivy into Billings all that time? Could she have been helping Ivy torture me? She was the only other person who had been in the room when Cheyenne had pulled her blush bead act. It all made perfect sense. And I knew she was still friendly with Ivy. She and Portia were the ones who had floated the idea of re-extending Ivy's invite to Billings at the beginning of the year. Maybe she had been trying to bring Ivy and Cheyenne back together. Smooth everything over. That was totally her style.

But then why would sweet little Rose want to stalk me? She had been Cheyenne's best friend. Did she really think I had pushed

Cheyenne over the edge? Was she punishing me? Did she blame me for Cheyenne's expulsion?

"Where is she?" I said, glancing over at the Billings table. "I have to talk to her."

"Rose? You didn't hear?" Sabine said, stabbing at a chunk of melon with her fork.

"Hear what?" I asked, my throat closing.

"She went home yesterday morning," Sabine replied. "She has mono or something, so they sent her home so she wouldn't spread it."

"Mono?" I repeated. That seemed a tad convenient. Right when I was onto a breakthrough, the girl who could sort it all out had fled campus? My pulse raced through my veins like a brakeless freight train. It was all too big of a coincidence. It had to be Rose and Ivy. It had to be.

But why?

"You should go to the police," Sabine said, her eyes serious. "I mean it, Reed. If someone is stalking you, that's a serious crime, no?"

I scoffed. "They won't listen to me. I've already asked them to investigate Ivy and they won't bother. I need to get some concrete evidence."

"Well, did you take pictures of the damage to your room?" Sabine asked. "Show them that."

My face burned in embarrassment. It hadn't even occurred to me to take pictures. I had been too busy freaking out and trying to clean it up so that I wouldn't have to look at it anymore.

"No. No pictures," I said.

"Oh." Sabine chewed slowly. "Well then, next time . . . I mean, if there is a next time," she said comfortingly, "make sure you get pictures."

"I will."

I folded my arms on the table and rested my chin atop them, realizing I actually felt relieved. Just like that, I could put Ivy back at the top of my list. I no longer had to figure out a whole new list of stalker suspects. I wouldn't have to look over my shoulder every second—only when Ivy was around.

Another laugh from the Billings table caught our attention. Sabine rolled her eyes as she took another bite of melon.

"I am so sick of that Amberly girl," she said.

"Tell me about it," I replied, happy for the change of subject. Something to distract me. "I'll bet she sucks as a roommate."

"I hardly know," Sabine replied. "She's in Noelle's room twenty-four-seven. They're fused at the hip. All they do is talk about their travel plans for Christmas. Noelle even gave Amberly a vintage Louis Vuitton travel trunk. Portia said it's worth more than Noelle's car."

I could practically feel my skin turning green. It was weird even to think about Portia and Sabine hanging around Billings, discussing such things. Weird to think that normal Billings life was going on without me.

"I don't understand what Noelle sees in her," I said through my teeth. "Would you believe the little twit tried to blackmail me?"

"No! How?" Sabine asked.

"Remember the other night at the library when you walked in on us by the vending machines?" I said.

Sabine nodded, obviously intrigued, her fork suspended over her fruit salad.

"She basically told me she wanted me to give her that Billings disc or else," I said, rolling my eyes.

Sabine's face slackened slightly. "But you destroyed that disc."

"I know, but I told Noelle I still had a copy," I replied, blushing slightly as I recalled my own lame attempt at blackmail.

"Oh. But you don't?" Sabine asked, pushing her food around now.

"No. I was just trying to get Noelle's attention," I said with a sigh, folding my arms on the table. "Anyway, Amberly went all *Sopranos* about it. Like she was willing to do anything to protect her own."

"Well, it's a good thing she can't get her hands on that information," Sabine said, laying her fork down finally. "It would not be good for anyone if that got out."

"I know. I kind of have a feeling that, no matter what she says, our privacy would not be her first priority," I added, glancing over at Amberly as she held out her hand to show her manicured nails to Lorna.

"A ditzy little upstart like her? Definitely not," Sabine agreed, following my gaze.

"Well, whatever. I'm kind of dying to see what her version of 'or else' looks like," I said with a laugh as I stood. "I'm going to go get some more cereal."

As I rejoined the food line, Ivy and Josh were just coming out the other end with their breakfasts. Much to my surprise, Josh said hi to me, but Ivy simply smirked. I narrowed my eyes at her and didn't look away until the snarky expression completely fell off her face.

She and Rose had been torturing me. I was sure of it. Now all I had to do was find the proof. And photograph it.

DIFFICULT

As I sat in morning services, listening to the Crom drone on about rules and regulations for tomorrow night's Easton Holiday Dinner, I realized I felt better than I had at breakfast. About as good as a person in my rather precarious and pathetic position could feel. I turned in my pew slightly to glance back at Noelle. She was texting on her iPhone, so she didn't see me. I couldn't help but cross my fingers. I so had to win her back tomorrow night. *Had* to. Because if my plan didn't work . . . No. I couldn't think that way. I had to be positive.

Wiping the worry from my mind, I started to face forward again, but before I could I caught a glimpse of Josh on the other side of the aisle, sitting on the end of the last pew. He wasn't paying attention to Cromwell either. Instead, he was sketching like crazy in a small sketch pad, his brow knit in intense concentration. As I watched him, he pressed his lips together, then pursed them, then went back

to normal and started the process all over again. I smiled, my eyes
stinging with nostalgia.

He always did that when he was really in the zone, though he never
believed me when I told him about it. I wished I could take a picture
right then and prove it to him, but it wasn't my place anymore. And
besides, Cromwell's henchman Mr. White would see the flash and
swoop down on me like a vulture.

But I couldn't tear my eyes away from Josh. The weak sunlight
streaming through the colorful stained-glass windows danced against
the right side of his face. There was a tiny fray in the hem of his turtleneck sweater and his corduroys were partially rolled up on one side,
revealing the tiniest bit of pale skin. I drank in every detail of him
while I could. If only he knew how much I missed every inch of him,
inside and out. If only he knew how much I regretted everything.

Cromwell dismissed us just as the second brilliant idea of the past
twenty-four hours hit me like a brick to the head. The perfect gift for
Josh. What might be the perfect gift for both of us.

I jumped up and raced down the rapidly filling aisle, headed for
the heavy, arched door. If I was going to pull this off, I was going to
need as much time as I could make for myself.

"Gotta throw up again, Brennan?" Ivy shouted after me. "They
have clinics for that kind of thing!"

A few people laughed, but I ignored them all. I would deal with Ivy
later. I shoved the door open and the cold air hit me like a slap to the
face. I paused for a second to button up and pull my hat on. Big, big
mistake.

"So, Glass-Licker," Amberly said, sidling up next to me. "You missed your deadline."

I clenched my jaw and started speed-walking down the cobbled path. Unfortunately, Amberly had no trouble keeping up.

"You owe me a disc, remember?" she said. "I hope you have it with you this morning. I'm really too busy to keep following you around."

I stopped in my tracks and looked at her, letting out a fed-up sigh.

"You don't have it, do you?" Amberly laughed and shook her head. "Don't you realize I can make things very difficult for you?"

I threw up my hands and let them slap down at my sides. "Do you even hear how ridiculous you sound? What did you do last summer, take some course called Soap Opera Villainy 101?"

Amberly's blue eyes narrowed. She tugged her fur-lined gloves on slowly. "Okay, then. Difficult it is."

I shook my head mirthfully. "Yes. Difficult it is. Bring on the difficult. I can't *wait* to see what your tiny little brain comes up with."

Then I turned and strolled off casually, letting her see just how very unaffected I was by her threats. There was a lot that could get to me, especially lately, but I was not going to be intimidated by some poser freshman. Especially not Amberly.

EVIDENCE

I spent the next twenty-four hours on edge. Not only was I now looking forward to the Holiday Dinner as the potential setting for my reconciliation with both Noelle *and* Josh, but I was dying to get back into Ivy's room and do some more snooping. I had to find some real evidence that she was my stalker and that she was plotting against Noelle. I had to put an end to her plans before I lost my mind. Before Noelle lost her life.

In the meantime, a thousand questions plagued me. Did Ivy really kill Cheyenne? And if so, did Rose know about it, or was she only helping Ivy mess with me? Why would Rose want to hurt Cheyenne? They had been such good friends. And why would she want to hurt Noelle?

Too many questions. None of which would be answered by Rose, apparently, since I had left about twenty messages on her voice mail and heard nothing back.

But no matter. I could take care of this without her explaining—or, even better, admitting her guilt. If I was on my own, I was on my own.

Friday morning I stood next to my door inside my room and waited for Ivy and Jillian to get their stuff together and get out. The general noise in the hallways was convivial and excited. The Crom had shortened all our classes for the day, so that they would all be crammed in before lunch, giving us time to get ready for the Holiday Dinner that afternoon. The atmosphere in Pemberly was not unlike the last day at Croton High before Christmas break. I could just tell no one was going to be paying attention in class. We would all be too busy looking forward to the festivities.

But first, I had a mission.

I heard Ivy and Jillian's door close and they strode by my room, chatting about what they might wear that night. Taking Sabine's advice to heart, I slid my iPhone into the back pocket of my jeans and waited until their voices faded to nothing. Then I slipped out of my room and into theirs. This time I went right for Ivy's dresser, yanking open the top drawer. All her things were folded and lined up in perfect little rows, the black underwear separated from the white, separated from the colorful. Crap. If I was going to search this stuff, I was going to have to do it carefully, meticulously. Not good, considering how badly my hands were shaking.

Taking a deep breath, I pushed a row of tiny undies aside, cringing at the very idea that I was touching Ivy Slade's intimates. I quickly uncovered birth control pills and a box of condoms, both of which

made me think of her and Josh and how far they might have already
gone, which made me want to vomit, but there was nothing else
there.

The second drawer was all T-shirts, again perfectly folded and
arranged in rows. I lifted out a stack and there was nothing underneath. Same with the next: o for 2.

The third drawer contained about twenty black and white sweaters.
Ivy's staples. I lifted up the first pile, holding the sweaters toward my
shoulder, and froze. Sitting in the bottom of the drawer was a very
familiar silver box. A box with the letters *VMS* etched into the lid. The
very box Ivy had been sent into her grandmother's house to steal. The
very box I had seen in Cheyenne's room the night before her parents
had come to pack up all her things.

Clutching the sweaters in the crook of my arm, I reached down
with my free hand and flipped open the lid of the box. Sure enough,
sitting inside on the velvet lining was Cheyenne's diamond *B*
necklace—which was slightly bigger than everyone else's—the chain
broken a few inches away from the clasp.

Ivy must have sneaked into Billings that night—the night before
Cheyenne's things were carted away. It was the only explanation. She
was still so angry that Cheyenne had taken the box, she must have
sneaked in to steal it back. That was how much this little token meant
to her.

Suddenly, my skin tingled with excitement. This was it. This was
the key. The heirloom box gave Ivy a very concrete motive. She had
never forgiven Cheyenne for her role in her grandmother's stroke and

for leaving her there to take the blame. She had never forgiven her for taking the family heirloom with her. So she had killed Cheyenne and, once she knew the police had inventoried everything, she had sneaked back to the scene of the crime to reclaim what was hers. The fact that the *B* necklace was inside was even better. Maybe Ivy had ripped it off of Cheyenne during some kind of struggle. I would have bet my life that the *B* had Ivy's fingerprints all over it.

This was it. I finally had her.

Fingers trembling, I whipped out my iPhone and snapped a picture of the open box with the *B* necklace inside, sitting right where it was. Then I covered my hand with the end of my sleeve to keep from leaving more fingerprints, closed the box, and snapped another picture. Finally, I took a step back and got the wider scene—the open drawer with the box inside and some of Ivy's things in the background, so that the police would have no question as to where I was.

I placed the sweaters back in the drawer and closed it carefully. My heart was racing with unbridled excitement. Ivy was going down. It was almost over. I almost couldn't believe it.

I was about to grab the doorknob and hightail it out of there, when I heard determined footsteps coming down the hall.

"So stupid," someone said to herself.

My heart stopped. It wasn't just someone. It was Ivy. She was about two seconds away from opening her door and finding me standing in the middle of her room with my iPhone out.

I wheeled around. The door to Jillian's closet was open. I flung myself inside, tripping on her shoes and banging into a dozen hangers, and yanked the door closed.

Ivy shoved the door to the room open and stormed inside. I was breathing so hard she was sure to hear me. I grasped the sleeve of one of Jillian's sweaters and held it over my mouth, forcing myself to breathe in and out slowly, quietly. Through the tiny space between door and wall, I could see Ivy moving about.

"Where the hell did I put it?" she said to herself, shoving some papers aside on her desk.

She groaned and opened a drawer, then slammed it. Shuffled a few more things around. The whole time I had to clutch myself to keep from trembling and losing my balance atop the sea of pumps and boots and sneakers. If I moved, my ankle might turn and I might tumble right out onto the floor.

That would be very not good.

"Ah! Thank God," Ivy said finally.

She shoved whatever she was looking for into her bag and strode past me toward the door. She got so close to the closet I could see the fur lining on her coat and smell her musky perfume. It was all I could do to keep from gagging. Then she walked out and slammed the door behind her.

I let out a breath but didn't move. Glancing at my Nike watch, I forced myself to wait. And wait. And wait. Until five full minutes had passed. Then I finally emerged from the closet and took a real breath.

"That was way too close," I said to myself.

I was about to flee the scene when something caught my eye and I paused. It was the picture—the photo of Cheyenne, Noelle, Ariana, and Ivy. It still hung above Ivy's bed, but something about it had changed. As I took a tentative step toward it, I realized what it was. Every single face had been X'd out with black marker except for Ivy's. Just like the photo of me and Cheyenne.

My whole body trembled. What did these defaced photos actually mean? Was she close to getting rid of Noelle? And if so, how did she intend to do it? Hands quaking, I lifted my phone and snapped a photo of the photo. Then I took a step back and snapped the wider scene once again.

This was all I needed. I was going to the police. And this time, they were going to have to listen to me. Noelle's life—and maybe even my own—depended on it.

"I'm sorry, Reed. I don't really know what you think this proves," Detective Hauer said, sliding my iPhone across the table to me. He pushed up the sleeves of his drab, tan sweater and folded his arms on the table in front of his notebook.

I felt as if every muscle in my body had just atrophied all at once. He had to be kidding me. First, the two officers at Hell Hall had told me that Detective Hauer wouldn't be on campus today. So then I had been forced to skip an entire morning of classes, sneak off campus, walk all the way over here in the freezing cold, and suffer on that cracked plastic chair in their saunalike waiting room for over an hour. All of that for him to just dismiss me?

"I already told you," I said, sitting forward until my upper body was pressed against the edge of the table, my hands clasped in my lap. "Ivy herself explained to me how much this silver box meant to her. To her, it's the reason her grandmother died. Cheyenne not only left her alone at her grandmother's that night to potentially watch the woman die, but she took the box with her. Ivy hated her for that."

"So she killed Cheyenne over a jewelry box," the detective said skeptically, leaning his elbow on the table and his chin on his hand. "That's not much of a motive."

"No! She killed Cheyenne over her grandmother's death!" I said, frustrated. "Look at the photos of Cheyenne's room from the morning we found her. That box is sitting on her desk. Now it's hidden in Ivy's room. She must have gone back and taken it. To her that box is a symbol of everything that happened that night. Maybe she thought that if you guys found it you might figure it all out. I mean, isn't that what guilty people do? Return to the scene of the crime to cover their tracks?"

The detective took a deep breath and glanced toward the open doorway behind me, toward the hustle and bustle of the office, as if he was wishing he was out there rather than in here. Why did he refuse to take me seriously?

"Listen, Reed, we've already talked to Ivy and she has an alibi for the night Cheyenne was murdered." He pulled his notebook toward him and flipped through it. "She was with Gage Coolidge all night and he corroborated her story."

"So? Gage is totally in love with Ivy," I protested. "He'd say anything she asked him to say."

Hauer looked at me with the expression of a man who was starting to get fed up with pandering to a whiny kindergartner. I wasn't sure whether I wanted to cry or smack him across his tired, old face. Instead, I whipped out my next weapon.

"Look," I said, pulling the destroyed photo of Cheyenne and me out of my bag and slapping it down in front of him. "I found this in my room the other day."

Detective Hauer picked up the two halves of the photo by their edges and looked them over. I grabbed my iPhone and scrolled to the pic of Ivy's photo, then turned it to him.

"Now look at this," I said. "Me, Cheyenne, Ariana, Noelle. All of us X'd out in the exact same way. The girl has already taken care of Cheyenne, and Ariana took care of herself. That leaves me and Noelle," I said, my voice trembling. "She's coming after us next, I swear."

For the first time all morning, Detective Hauer looked slightly interested. Even concerned. I was glad that the fact that I was afraid for my own life had actually gotten through to him. He had a heart after all. He placed the phone and the photo in front of him and studied them. I seized my moment.

"Is that what you want, Detective?" I asked. "Do you really want another murder on your hands?"

He lifted his weary eyes to me and sighed, then sat back in his chair.

"Crosby!" he shouted, so loud I actually jumped in my chair..

Almost instantly, a skinny guy in a blue uniform scrambled into the room. "Yes, Detective?"

"Grab an evidence bag and some gloves and get in here," he ordered. "I want this photo dusted for prints."

"Yes, sir," the cop said.

My heart leapt as I looked back at Detective Hauer. Was this for real? Was he finally going to help me?

"We'll look into it," he said, glancing at the picture on my iPhone once more. Glancing at it as if he didn't like what he saw. "I'm not guaranteeing anything, but we'll look into it."

IMMATURE STAMP

By the time I got back to campus after making a quick stop at the Hallmark store in town for some supplies to complete Josh's gift, classes were over for the day. Students were streaming out of the cafeteria following lunch and loitering on the quad before heading to their dorms to start primping and dressing and finishing wrapping their presents. The timing couldn't have been more perfect. If I had strolled back onto campus an hour earlier, I could have easily been snagged for skipping, but now I blended right in.

Praying I wouldn't bump into Ivy on my way back to my room lest I give away my anticipatory glee, I took the stairs instead of the elevator. My plan was to hunker down alone in my dorm for the rest of the afternoon and wait to see what happened next. If the police did come to arrest Ivy, I wanted to be there to witness it.

I speed-walked down the hall to my room, tugging my scarf from my neck and unbuttoning my coat. There were a few girls hanging out in front of their rooms, but Ivy wasn't among them. When I slipped inside, I turned around and closed the door, allowing myself a quick breath of relief. Home free.

Then I turned and faced my room. A gasp of horror escaped my throat.

The place was a complete wreck. The drawers of my dresser yawned open, clothes spilling out of them and covering the entire floor. My bed was unmade, pillows on the floor as well. My closet was open and half the clothes inside had been ripped from the hangers. The Chloé bag had been tossed in the corner, unclasped and upside down. Two of the three posters Constance had given me had been slashed in half and the third hung from one sorry tack over my bed. Even the photo of Scott and me hadn't come through unscathed. The glass was broken and the frame cracked.

I was going to kill Ivy. I was going to *kill* her.

My hands had just curled into fists when I noticed that all my CDs were fanned out across the desk, some of them having tumbled to the floor.

CDs. Wait a second. CDs.

Maybe this wasn't Ivy's handiwork after all.

I grabbed the Chloé bag and righted it, then yanked open the small, inside pocket. It was empty.

"Amberly," I said through my teeth. "You little bitch."

She hadn't found the Billings disc, which, of course, didn't exist. But she had managed to find her precious Carma Card. Plus what was left of my Billings fund money. Both were gone from their hiding place inside the Chloé bag.

My heart rate started to return to normal as my brain accepted the fact that this had not been the work of my stalker. There was nothing Cheyenne-related about this particular attack. No. Amberly had done this. The pointless destruction had her immature stamp all over it. Apparently, this was her idea of "doing things the difficult way."

I groaned as I looked around at the disaster area that was my room, hating the fact that Amberly had—even in a tiny way—gotten the better of me. Part of me wanted to storm right over to Billings and steal the stupid Carma Card right back, just to prove a point, but I knew that was never going to happen. No one over there was going to let me through the front door, let alone allow me to ransack my old room. I hated that Amberly had managed to get into my room and mess with me, but there was nothing I could do about it now. I wasn't going to let that twit ruin the rest of my day—the day on which Ivy might finally be arrested, the day on which I might finally get through to Noelle and Josh.

No. I was just going to have to deal. And hopefully, by the end of the night, this mess would turn out to be just a blip in an otherwise perfect day.

MUCH WORSE

"I cannot believe she did this to you," Sabine said, shaking her head as she speed-folded my clothes and stacked them into my dresser. Apparently, when Sabine was angry, she was like a whirling dervish. In five minutes she had cleaned up all the clothes, hanging them back in their places and tucking them into drawers. "That's it. I'll never talk to that girl again."

I smiled wanly as I carefully removed the photo of Scott and me from the broken frame. "Thanks, but won't that make your living situation a tad difficult?"

"I don't care," Sabine said, shoving the drawer closed. "Clearly there is something wrong with this girl. You can't just break into people's rooms. What is wrong with everyone?"

Good question. I was about to attempt an answer when several male voices filled the hallway. I heard the telltale feedback from a walkie-talkie and my heart skipped a beat. Sabine and I locked eyes.

I felt tingles all over every inch of my skin. This was it. They had come for Ivy.

"Yes, sir. I understand," Headmaster Cromwell's voice echoed down the hall. "I understand that, but I have the academy's lawyer right here and she has looked over the warrant. Everything appears to be in order."

Quaking with excitement and uncertainty, I crept over to my door and cracked it open. Two uniformed police officers strode by my room along with the Crom, who was on his cell, and a rotund woman in a gray suit who was reading over some legal document. Bringing up the rear was Detective Hauer in his thick wool coat, looking grim. The officers stopped and one of them knocked on Ivy's door. His blue vinyl jacket swished with every movement he made.

"Ms. Slade? Ms. Crane? This is the Easton Police Department."

"What's going on?" Sabine asked, trying to see through the crack by leaning into my shoulder from behind.

I closed the door quietly and looked at her, wide-eyed. "It's the police. They've come for Ivy!" I whispered.

My God. They must have found her fingerprints on my photo. I had finally done something right.

"Right now?" Sabine asked, clutching her hands together.

"What's going on?" I heard Ivy ask from next door.

"Shhh!" I said to Sabine, putting my hands out and freezing in place as if doing so would help me hear better. All up and down the hall, doors were opening and closing as my floor mates checked out the drama.

"Miss Slade, we have a warrant to search your things," one of the officers said.

"What? What for?" Ivy blurted, sounding angry.

"Yes, sir. Yes. She's right here," Headmaster Cromwell said.

He must have handed Ivy the phone, because in the next second I could hear her rambling right outside my door.

"Daddy! Yes, there are three of them and they're going through all my stuff! What is going on?"

She sounded on the verge of tears. I would have given anything to have been able to open my door, but everyone was crowded right outside. My appearance would have been way too obvious. So all I could do was stand there and imagine. Imagine how scared Ivy must have looked as she realized she was finally about to be brought to justice.

There was another squeal of the walkie-talkie and a voice came through. "Detective Hauer, sir, we have the Coolidge boy. Should we take him right to the car?"

"Gage?" Sabine mouthed.

"Yes, Officer Crosby. We'll meet you there as soon as we wrap this up," Detective Hauer responded.

My pulse pounded in my ears. Now that this was all happening, it seemed so very out of control. Had they decided that Gage was some kind of accomplice? Was I right in guessing that he had lied to the police to protect Ivy? I actually felt a thump of guilt at the thought of Gage being dragged off campus by the police. Who knew I had any sort of soft spot in my heart for that jerk?

"Miss Slade? Care to explain this?" Detective Hauer asked.

"What? Dad, hang on," Ivy said. There was a pause. "Wait a minute. Who did this?" Ivy asked.

"Are you trying to tell me you didn't deface this photo yourself?" Detective Hauer said.

"No! No, I didn't," Ivy said. "I have no idea who did that, but it wasn't me."

I rolled my eyes at her obvious lie. That was it. I couldn't take this anymore. I opened the door and stood in the doorway with Sabine just behind me. Everyone looked over at us. Headmaster Cromwell with his pinched expression. Ivy, looking waxy and pale, clutching the cell phone through which her father was barking orders. Detective Hauer, holding the X'd-out photo of Cheyenne, Noelle, Ariana, and Ivy in his gloved hand. Even the lawyer lady looked me up and down.

"Miss Brennan, Miss DuLac. This is not a theater matinee," Headmaster Cromwell said bitterly, crossing his arms over his chest. "Kindly wait inside."

"Fine. I just want to say one thing to Ivy," I told him. Then I looked her in the eye. Looked right at the girl who had spent the last two months doing everything she could think of to ruin my life, and slowly smiled. "I hope you get everything that's coming to you," I said firmly.

Her jaw dropped slightly, and her eyes filled with confusion and ire. But I didn't care. I just slammed my door right in her face.

"Wow. That was cold," Sabine said.

"She deserves it," I told Sabine, my tone grim. "For everything she's done to me, to Cheyenne . . . she deserves much worse."

That night I hummed to myself as I put the final touches on my new-and-improved gift for Josh. I hadn't felt so at peace in my room since moving into Pemberly. In fact, I had lived a long while in Billings without feeling this calm and secure. But now, the police finally had my stalker in custody. For the first time in weeks, I was certain that nothing bad could happen. For the first time in weeks I felt truly free.

I was washing my hands of this mess. Ivy was now officially the problem of the Easton Police Department.

I slipped Josh's gift into the small red box I had purchased at the stationery store that afternoon, then affixed the glossy white bow to the top. Satisfied that I had done the best I could, I turned and checked myself out in the mirror on the back of my door. I smiled at my reflection. My long brown hair was pinned up on one side, while the other fell in sultry waves over my shoulder. I wore black mascara and dark red lip gloss I had picked up on that fateful fund-raiser weekend in New York. Sparkling in my earlobes were the diamond earrings Walt Whittaker had given me last year. The effect was totally simple and totally glam. But the best part was the dress. I was wearing the red Nicole Miller dress Portia had bought for me all those weeks ago. It had only been worn once before, when I'd gone on that awful date with Hunter Braden, and I had a feeling he wouldn't remember it at all, considering how very self-absorbed he was. The Billings Girls would all remember it, of course, and that was exactly how I wanted it. Wearing this dress meant they hadn't beaten me. Wearing this dress meant I had risen above.

I just hoped Portia didn't try to tear it off me like the ugly step-sisters had done to Cinderella. That would not be pretty.

There was a knock at the door and I quickly opened it. Sabine and Constance stood in the hallway, cuddled into their long wool coats. Constance's red hair was pulled back from her face with wisps hanging down around her cheeks, and she wore more eye makeup than I had ever seen her attempt before. Sabine was looking as natural as ever, but she had woven a small braid into her hair on the right side and clasped it with a tiny rhinestone clip.

"Reed, you look gorgeous," Sabine gushed, looking me up and down.

"Ready to party?" Constance asked, pushing herself up on her toes in excitement.

A little thrill ran right through my chest. This was the first night of the rest of my life. I grabbed Josh's gift and my coat on my way out the door.

"You have no idea how ready."

THE EASTON HOLIDAY DINNER

"So, is anyone making a toast?" Constance asked, taking a sip of red punch.

"No way," Sonal replied with a snort. "I could never get up in front of the entire school and do that."

"I know. Me neither," Constance said. "Worst nightmare."

Much to my shock, Constance had stayed by my side for the entire cocktail hour—or mocktail hour, I suppose, since only sodas, punch, and sparkling cider were served. Maybe Sabine's bravery was rubbing off on her. Whatever the cause, I appreciated it. In fact, before long I was surrounded by friends. Constance, Sabine, Marc, Astrid, Diana, Sonal, Shane. For a leper I was doing quite well for myself.

"Really getting a lot of mileage out of that dress, aren't you, Reed?" Shelby asked, looking me up and down with a sneer as she, Portia, and the Twin Cities strolled by. Shelby was wearing a royal blue dress I had never seen before, with an asymmetrical, off-the-shoulder neckline and full skirt.

"It *is* the only one she's got," Portia added. She was, as ever, sporting her signature green—a slim-cut dress that showed off every single curve.

There was definitely a comeback in there. Something about how Portia only ever wore the same nasty color, but they sidled off before I could respond, laughing happily at their lame insults.

Okay. So maybe I wasn't doing *perfectly* well.

"Ignore those cows," Astrid said, laying a cold hand on my bare arm. She was as funky as ever in a punked-out pink dress with black and purple netting over the skirt and a pillbox hat. Her shoes were black lace high-top Converse. "Instead, let's discuss how the Crom has completely transformed the cafeteria. I expect it took him ages to plan all this. Perhaps he has a soft side after all."

"I kind of doubt the last part, but it is pretty spectacular," I admitted.

On every window hung a real fir wreath decorated with pinecones and red ribbons, and real evergreen swags were draped along the walls, strung with white lights as well, filling the room with the comforting scent of fresh pine. All the chairs were covered in green velvet and secured with red bows, and at each china place setting was a small favor of Godiva chocolate, presented in a little red sleigh. But the real main attraction was the clothes. The students of Easton definitely knew how to clean up. Everywhere I looked there were velvet frocks and pearls, wrist-length gloves and kitten heels, tuxes and silk scarves. It was one big constant-motion fashion show. Even the flasks the guys were hiding in the pockets of their jackets were superchic. Monogrammed or platinum or leather or, in Dominic Infante's case, Gucci.

And then, of course, there was the tremendous Christmas tree in the center of the room. The star at the top nearly brushed the panes of the skylight, and every sparkling ornament on the tree was perfectly placed. White lights twinkled and winked from its boughs, and the garland was made of hand-strung popcorn and cranberries.

"Do you think the garland is real?" I asked.

"It is. I already checked," Marc said, popping an hors d'oeuvre into his mouth.

"How did you check?" Constance asked.

Marc turned pink and shrugged one shoulder. "I ate a kernel."

Everyone laughed and I let myself bask in the total peace and tranquility of the moment. For the first time in so long I felt normal. I felt social. I felt warm. Over by the tree, students were lining up to add their gifts to the pile, which was now overflowing into the aisle between tables in both directions.

"So, who did you get in the gift thing?" Astrid asked me.

I glanced at Marc, who looked quickly away. "I'll never tell," I replied.

"Oh, rubbish! It's over now. You have to tell," Astrid wheedled.

I blushed and shook my head. The last thing I wanted was for all my friends to be watching Josh when he opened his present. "Nope! Never!"

"God. I wish I had been there," Sonal whispered behind me.

"Been there for what?" I asked, tuning in and hoping to distract Astrid.

Sonal looked at Diana and Shane as if she had been snagged.

"When they dragged Ivy off," Shane answered for her. "Did you see anything?"

I glanced around to see if anyone was listening in, then took a step closer to Sonal, drawing the entire group into a tighter circle. I had never been big on gossip and rumors, but for once there was a story I was dying to spread. If only because this story might finally prove to everyone that I was innocent.

"Not much," I admitted. "But Sabine and I heard the whole thing. It sounded like they were pretty convinced she had something to do with Cheyenne's death."

Of course, I'd heard nothing of the sort. But I knew what I knew.

"The girl is definitely guilty," Sabine put in. "You could see it all over her face."

"You must be freaking out, Reed," Constance said. "I mean, Josh is *dating* her."

"I know," I replied, my heart sinking.

I looked over my shoulder again and immediately found Josh in the mingling throng. I had been paying attention to his where-abouts all night. He had been sticking close to his usual crowd—Trey, Weston Bright, and the other guys from Ketlar—and seemed to be having a good time, considering his girlfriend was in police custody. Was it because he couldn't care less about Ivy, or because he was so convinced that nothing would come of it? So convinced of her innocence.

Oh, how I hoped it was the former.

"Well, at least it gets you off the rumor mill," Diana said with a small smile. "You must be happy about that."

"You have no idea," I told her with a laugh.

Soon everyone would know that I was innocent. Soon Noelle and Josh would realize that I had been right all along. That I had saved them both from being hurt. Soon everything would be back the way it was supposed to be.

Well, almost the way it was supposed to be. I spotted Amberly on the other side of the room, wearing a light blue sheath and holding court with Missy and Lorna. With her around, there would be no room for me in Billings, even if Noelle miraculously decided to forgive me. Part of me wanted to grab the cocktail sauce from a passing waiter's tray, go over there, and dump it over her platinum blond head—get back at her for destroying my room the way she had, for invading my privacy, trashing my things, trying to take my place. But I simply clenched my fingers and told myself to chill. Now was not the time or the place. There was always tomorrow for a catfight. Tonight I was focusing on the positive.

A sudden tinkle of silver bells brought the conversation in the room to a complete halt. Headmaster Cromwell stepped up in front of the tree. For a man who had just watched two of his students get hauled off by the cops, he was looking calm and composed. Happy, even.

"If everyone will take your seats, the first course is about to be served," he announced, with the proud air of someone who was pulling off the event of the season.

"I'll see you guys later?" I said to Marc, Sabine, and the other Billings Girls.

"Definitely," Constance replied.

With a smile, I wove my way toward the Pemberly table with Diana, Shane, and Sonal. It was so nice to feel as if I had friends again. But at the same time, my heart started to pound with trepidation. The start of the meal meant that the moment of truth was coming. I hugged myself and hoped that I was prepared. Before long, my fate would be decided.

GUTS

"So I just want to say 'Hells, yeah' to the members of the men's soccer team!" Trey announced, gesturing so vehemently with his right hand that his sparkling cider sloshed over the side of the glass in his left. "Thanks for the most kick-ass senior season ever!"

The members of the team, peppered throughout the room, went wild, and everyone else joined in, cheering for Trey's toast as he downed his drink. Headmaster Cromwell, however, didn't look all that pleased.

"Thank you, Mr. Prescott," he said, stepping up behind Trey and laying a heavy hand on his shoulder. "That was very eloquent," he said sarcastically.

Trey glanced at the headmaster, chagrined, and dropped into his chair. Across the table from Trey, Josh shook his head and smirked. The speech was kind of out of character for one of the most mature guys on campus. I wondered if Trey had brought along his own flask, or if he had been sipping from someone else's.

"And now, moving on to Pemberly . . ." Headmaster Cromwell stepped up to the end of our table. My breath caught in my throat and instantly, my body temperature doubled. This was it. Now or never. "Would any of the Pemberly ladies care to make a toast?"

Everyone at the table glanced at everyone else. I was just starting to think it might be wise to wait for someone else to go first, when it became clear that no one had any intention of saying a thing. I suppose the women of Pemberly weren't exactly an extroverted crowd. Headmaster Cromwell's lips pursed in annoyance, and suddenly I found myself raising my hand at table level.

"I have something to say."

Instantly, murmurs sprung up at all the surrounding tables and quickly spread the length and breadth of the room. My heart started to pound in earnest.

"What's *she* going to say?" Amberly whispered. "'Thanks for letting me get away with murdering one of my friends?'"

Right. So even though the news of Ivy's arrest had spread across campus like a bad stomach flu, I guess not everyone believed in her guilt quite yet. I had expected the headmaster to be relieved that Pemberly wasn't going to entirely let him down. Instead, his face clouded over. I really was not his favorite person on campus.

"Fine, then," he said gruffly. He lifted his chin and announced to the room, "Miss Reed Brennan would like to make a toast!"

The level of buzz in the room grew as I awkwardly pushed my chair back and stood. This was it. My big, brilliant win-Noelle-back plan. I had publicly humiliated her with the Dash video. The only way I could think of to make up for it was to publicly praise her.

My knees were quaking like a Jell-O mold in an earthquake, and for the first time, I was annoyed with myself for not bringing my notes along. I had thought it would be more sincere if I spoke from the heart, without the aid of index cards. But now that I could see the disapproving faces at the Billings table, I couldn't remotely recall what I'd been going to say.

My heart pounded quick and shallow. Everyone here was against me. I couldn't do this. What was I thinking? In about two seconds people were going to start hurling half-eaten rolls at me.

Then I looked at Noelle. She was watching me with amused interest, her arm crooked over the back of her chair, her legs crossed at the knee, the full, scalloped skirt of her black dress draping elegantly toward the floor. This was for her. I had to remember that. This was all for her.

"I would like to toast Noelle Lange," I announced in a loud, clear voice.

That *really* got the room going. Chairs squeaked, people laughed, incredulous voices filled the room. How was I ever going to get them to shut up? I glanced at Sabine helplessly, but her mouth was hanging open in total shock. Constance and Astrid looked blown away as well. All right, so I hadn't warned them that this was coming, but couldn't they understand? Didn't they know that sometimes a girl just had to lay it all on the line?

"Excuse me!" Headmaster Cromwell shouted. "I expect the same silence and courtesy for each and every one of your schoolmates!"

A hush fell on the cafeteria. An energized, anticipatory hush, but a hush nonetheless. Noelle reached for her water glass, took a non-chalant sip, and replaced it on the tablecloth before returning her attention to me, one eyebrow raised. I could just imagine what she was thinking:

This should be interesting.

I cleared my throat and began.

"As many of you . . . well, *all* of you, know, this has been a rather insane and traumatic semester for me. For a lot of us," I said. "There has been a lot of grief, a lot of upheaval, a lot of rumors—some very true, some very false," I said, the words of my preplanned speech coming back to me in a rush. "But I'm not here to defend myself or clear my name. I think that will come in its own time. I'm here to say that I would never have gotten through any of it without the friendship of Noelle Lange."

Noelle shifted in her seat ever so slightly. I was getting through to her. I had to be.

"Noelle is a true friend. She is someone who always has your back. Someone who will do anything for you if you need her. Someone who is creative and good and kind."

At this point I looked Noelle right in the eye. My palms were sweating so badly I was afraid I was going to drop my champagne flute, but I pressed on.

"And I'm sorry if I forgot all that for five stupid minutes. I'm sorry to have thrown away something so precious to me, over something so superficial. A friendship that could have lasted my whole life, over something so fleeting."

From the corner of my eye, I could see that everyone at the Billings table was either gaping at me or at Noelle. But the two of us simply stared at each other.

"So here's to Noelle Lange," I said, raising my glass. "A true asset to Billings, a true asset to Easton, and the true friend I hope will forgive me someday."

There was a prolonged moment of silence. I think everyone was so stunned they forgot where they were.

"To Noelle Lange!" Headmaster Cromwell announced finally, raising his glass. Not so much to save me, I'm sure, but to save his ceremony.

"Noelle Lange!" the room echoed.

We all sipped our drinks and I stood there, waiting for a reaction from Noelle. Waiting for any kind of sign. She simply sipped her sparkling cider and looked at me as if she was seeing me for the first time. Then she finally turned back to her table, turning her shoulder to me. That was it. No smile. No nod. Nothing.

I dropped into my chair, exhausted, and placed my glass back down on the table. I felt numb all over. As if my skin, my muscles, my bones, had all turned to dust.

"Damn, girl. That took guts," Shane said in my ear.

"But it wasn't enough," I said quietly, the realization seeping into my veins like poison. "Nothing's ever going to be enough."

CHRISTMAS WISHES

After Noelle's nonreaction to my speech, all I really wanted to do was retreat to Pemberly and sleep, but Headmaster Cromwell had made it clear this was a mandatory event, so I was in it for the long haul. I sat through coffee and dessert without touching a thing, but no one noticed my dejected state. Because after a few polite bites were taken, the student body got down to the real business of the night—hunting for their gifts. Once a few sophomore girls got up and ventured tentatively toward the tree, half the room was out of their seats and clamoring for their presents.

Suddenly I felt the mildest sizzle of excitement. The night wasn't over yet. I stood up as the rest of my table emptied, trying to keep an eye on Josh. Unfortunately, it took about two seconds for me to lose him in the mayhem.

"Reed? Aren't you coming?" Diana asked me as she pushed her chair in.

"Nah. I think I'll wait out the rush," I told her.

In truth, I had almost zero interest in finding my gift. Aside from a very select few, most of the people on this campus had been shunning me for days. What if whoever had drawn my name had gotten me some kind of gag gift? Like a box full of coal or a dead rat or something. I wasn't sure I'd be able to handle that with any kind of grace.

So instead, I sat back and watched. I watched as people tore through designer paper and whipped open gift boxes. Watched as the girls draped ribbons around one another's shoulders and *ooh*ed and *aah*ed over their gifts. I saw quite a few pairs of leather gloves, cashmere scarves, sparkly earrings, and Dooney & Bourke bags. There were also a few creative and fun gifts. A sleek remote-control helicopter that was soon winging its way around the room, threatening to take out the lights. An alarm clock that wouldn't break or stop beeping even if hurled across the room, a claim which was immediately tested by its new owner. One girl screeched so loudly when she opened her gift— a pair of front-row tickets to some sold-out concert—that everyone stopped for a minute and laughed.

Where was Josh? I was dying to see his reaction to his gift. To see if he understood the significance of the paintbrushes—the same ones we'd used last year to fling paint all over his dorm room walls. It had been the first time I'd realized just how much I cared about him. How much he understood me. Loved me. But Josh was nowhere to be found.

Feeling desperate now, I finally moved from my safety zone and did a slow lap of the room, staying on the outskirts by the tables—

never really approaching the tree. I found Trey and West checking out their new Nintendo DS systems, which had each come with a pile of games, but Josh wasn't with them. Had he left before the gift opening had begun? Had he taken one look at who his gift was from and tossed it in the nearest garbage can?

Soon the crowd around the tree began to disperse and I could tell there were only a couple dozen gifts left. Tentatively, I approached, wanting to check to see if Josh's present was still there. I walked around the tree slowly, carefully, stepping over crushed balls of wrapping paper and discarded packaging. I didn't see the small red box anywhere. Neither did I see anything intended for me.

Even though I had been prepared for the worst, I still felt a pang. Ostracized again. Left out of a huge tradition. Whoever had found my name in their mailbox had simply decided not to bother.

"Reed! Reed!"

I looked up to find Constance skipping toward me, her face flushed with excitement. She was waving a white envelope in front of her excitedly, like it contained all the answers to all the questions on all the finals we would ever take. She stopped short in front of me, nearly slipping on some fallen tissue paper, and held the envelope out with both hands.

"From your secret Santa," she said with a huge smile.

My name was written across the front of the envelope. I recognized Noelle's elegant handwriting instantly.

"What is it?" I said, half scared, half elated.

"Just open it," Constance whispered giddily.

I tore into the envelope and extracted a square white card. An invitation. To Noelle and Amberly's pre-Kiran's-birthday party the following night. My heart expanded so fast I thought I was going to burst.

"She just gave it to me and said to find you," Constance explained, coming over to my side so she could read the invite over my shoulder. "You did it, Reed. You're so back in!"

My fingers trembled as I looked at the card in disbelief. "Wait, did she always have my name, or did she trade with someone after she heard my speech?"

"Who cares?" Constance blurted happily. "You're coming to the party. We're all going to Kiran's together. Who cares how it happened?"

The girl had a point. I looked up, scanning the room for Noelle, and found her chatting with some of the Billings Girls over near their table. She glanced over at me as if she knew I was looking, and I held the card up and smiled. In return, she granted me a quick nod of acknowledgment, then refocused on her conversation.

It wasn't much, but it was something.

"I'm so happy for you!" Constance cried, grabbing me up in a hug.

"Me too," I replied with a smile.

Now if I could just find Josh, just hear what he had to say . . . maybe all my Christmas wishes would come true.

A NEW CURVE

Shane had received a huge, glossy, hardcover book on the history of Hollywood as her gift, which turned out to be lucky for all of us because it gave us something to block the wind with on the way back to Pemberly. It whipped around us like a cyclone, knocking us one way and then the other as we staggered toward the dorm.

"What is this, Kansas?" Diana joked, holding her hat down with both hands.

"Yeah. Arctic Kansas," Sonal added, cracking the others up.

I smiled and clutched the invitation from Noelle inside my coat pocket. I couldn't wait to get upstairs and look it over again. Make sure it wasn't written in disappearing ink or something. Make sure it was real.

A few yards from the back door of our dorm, we all noticed a tall, burly police officer standing just outside, bundled up in a long coat, scarf, and gloves, his silver shield glinting on his hat. My heart skipped a nervous beat. Our steps slowed.

"Ladies," the officer said with a nod. His voice was low and rumbling, his dark skin lined with age. "Kindly have your IDs ready to show to the officer inside."

I glanced at Diana and saw that my own fear was reflected in her eyes. What had happened now?

"Ooookay," Shane said, whipping out her key card.

She opened the door and let us all go in ahead of her. Just inside the lobby was another officer sitting at a small wooden table that used to stand under the far window. With his shaggy brown hair and squinty eyes darting everywhere, he reminded me of a nervous mouse. A laptop was open on the table in front of him, and he looked at us briefly as we approached, before his eyes darted away again.

"IDs, please," he said, holding out a skinny hand.

"What's this all about?" I asked.

He sighed, clearly irritated, and flicked his fingers. Didn't look any of us in the eye. "IDs?"

As we were fishing our wallets out of our pockets, the front door directly across from us opened and in walked Ivy Slade. I felt all the blood rush out of my head at the sight of her, and the flutter of fear I had felt outside returned with a vengeance. What was she doing back here? Why had they let her go?

Ivy spotted me as she strode by, her eyes narrowed in anger. She said something under her breath but kept right on moving to the elevator. I could hardly breathe. She was back. The stalking, murdering bitch was back. They'd only held her for three hours. And when I got upstairs, she would be right next door. Why had I even bothered going to Detective Hauer? Was this all some kind of massive joke to him?

I heard a familiar voice just as the cop at the table snatched my ID from my numb fingers to check it against his computer file. Detective Hauer had walked through the door and was conversing with another officer.

"Detective," I said, my voice cracking.

He looked up and his expression grew instantly weary. Like he so didn't want to deal with me. Well, life was tough. I so didn't want to deal with living next door to a psychopath.

"What are you doing?" I said through my teeth as I approached him. "How could you let her go?"

Detective Hauer squeezed his brow between his thumb and fore-finger for a moment before responding.

"I've told you before and I'll tell you again. She's not our girl," he replied.

"But what about the photos? And the box?" I blurted.

"They didn't hold a candle to the depositions we've been taking all afternoon and evening," Detective Hauer replied, pulling me toward the cozy seating area off to the side of the lobby. "We found dozens of people to corroborate her alibi, Reed. She and this Coolidge kid stayed at the Driscoll Hotel that night. We have bell-boys, maids, managers," he said, lifting his hand to tick them off on his fingers. "Room service receipts signed by her. There's a security tape that's being reviewed as we speak. Ivy Slade had nothing to do with Cheyenne Martin's death."

I was so stunned my face stung from the shock of it. I had been so certain. The girl had the best motive ever. Plus her behavior . . . the threats, the icy looks, the attitude, that freaky photo in her room. It all added up.

"Well . . . what about the picture I gave you?" I asked. "I still say she's stalking me and maybe Noelle, too."

"Her fingerprints weren't found on the print you supplied," Hauer told me in a soothing way. "And she swears she didn't deface her own photo. However, we did find traces of white wool fibers on both prints."

My heart seized. "What does that mean?"

"It means that the same person probably tampered with both pictures and wore white wool gloves while doing it," Hauer told me. "It appears as if you and Ms. Slade have the same stalker. This person is really getting around."

At that I leaned back on the rear of the couch behind me. There was no way I could wrap my brain around this. My stalker was also stalking Ivy? How was that even possible? Who on this campus had a vendetta against the two of us? We were enemies. We hated each other. Why would anyone lump us together?

Ivy was a victim too. That might have been the hardest fact of all to swallow. From murderous stalker to hunted victim in less than two minutes. At least this exonerated Rose. If Ivy was innocent, so was she.

"That's why we've stationed officers at each door and inside your building," Detective Hauer explained gently. "Until we catch this person and ensure that both you and Ivy are safe, the only people allowed through to the elevators and stairs will be the registered residents of Pemberly."

"I don't believe this," I said, sweating inside my wool coat. "I really don't believe this."

"I'm sorry," Detective Hauer said, pushing his hands into his coat pockets. "But don't worry. We're not going to let anything happen to you or to Ivy. We're going to figure out who's doing all this. I swear."

"Thanks," I said wanly.

"Reed? Are you coming?" Diana asked, hovering in the lobby with the others. She held up my ID, which I'd left with the check-in officer.

"Yeah. I guess," I replied. I pushed myself away from the couch, feeling weak, and looked up at Detective Hauer. "Thanks."

"Good night, Reed," he replied, trying for a bolstering smile.

I turned to my dorm mates, my shoulders rounded, and we all crowded into an elevator. They grilled me, of course, on what was going on, and I explained to them briefly, shocking the crap out of all of them. But I guess it couldn't be a secret anymore. Someone was after me. And apparently they were after Ivy, too. These girls deserved to know why Pemberly had been put on red alert.

"Sorry, guys," I said, as the elevator stopped on my floor and I stepped out. "This whole police presence thing is all my fault."

"Don't worry about it. Gives me something new to blog about," Shane said, waving a hand.

"Let me know if you need anything," Diana added.

Then the doors slid closed and they were gone.

I turned and trudged down the hallway to my room. All along the way, dorm room doors were open and the girls inside were whispering in hushed tones, trying to figure out what was going on. I didn't have the energy to stop and tell any of them what I knew. My brain was completely fried. Everything I had thought was true had turned out to be false. And Ivy being stalked as well? That was a curve I had not remotely considered.

I took a deep breath and opened the door to my room. Ivy Slade was sitting in my desk chair, facing the door, her legs crossed at the knee and her arms crossed in front of her.

"Oh, good. You're here," she said, getting up and brushing right by me to slam the door and sequester us in. "You and I are long overdue for a chat."

TWO HEADS

"So!" Ivy said, striding into the center of my room before turning to face me. She tilted her head to the side. "I hear you think I killed Cheyenne."

"They told you I was the one who turned you in?" I asked, stunned.

"No. Of course not. But the Easton PD isn't exactly a crack outfit," she said sarcastically. "I overheard at least five different people mention your name. So, what? Please tell me what you think would ever motivate me to kill the best friend I ever had."

I turned away from her and unbuttoned my coat with trembling fingers, stalling for time. What was I supposed to say to the girl?

The truth. It was clearly time for the truth.

I slipped my coat off, shivering in my flimsy dress, and faced her. We were a mere two feet away from each other, thanks to the tight quarters.

"You're the one who told me how much you hated Billings," I explained. "It was so obvious that you blamed Noelle and Ariana and Cheyenne for your grandmother's death. I figured you finally got your revenge. Plus you're always talking about how Noelle is going to get what's coming to her and how you're going to bring us all down. You threaten my friends every chance you get!"

Ivy laughed and shook her head, as if I were just so naïve. "That's just talk, Reed."

"Yeah right," I snapped back. "You have done a few sketchy things since I've known you, Ivy. Ostracizing Easton from the Legacy, trying to take down our fund-raiser. Come on. How was I supposed to know those threats were empty?"

She actually appeared to be pondering this. Seeing my point. She reached over to my dresser and toyed with one of the branches on the mini Christmas tree Sabine had given me, avoiding my gaze.

"And what the hell do you mean, the best friend you ever had? You hated Cheyenne," I added.

Ivy snorted a laugh and tipped her head forward for a moment to look at the floor. "Maybe at the end, but that doesn't mean I completely forgot about ten years of friendship. Haven't you ever had a love-hate relationship?"

My mind immediately flashed on Noelle, but I said nothing.

"So that's what you based this whole thing on?" she asked, lifting her pointy shoulders. "A couple of stupid pranks I pulled and some story I told you at the fund-raiser?"

My heart quivered nervously. Here it was. The moment of truth.

"No. That wasn't all," I said. I leaned back against my desk chair and braced myself. "I kind of snuck into your room and found the jewelry box and the broken necklace and the photo of you guys with all the faces X'd out but yours."

"You went through my stuff!?" Ivy shouted. She turned and put her hands on top of her head as if she were trying to keep her brain from exploding. "Oh my God. Forget Cheyenne. I might just have to kill *you*!"

"Ivy, you've gotta understand," I said, sounding desperate, and hating that I sounded desperate. I could not believe that I had been put in the position of begging for forgiveness from this girl. It was like the whole world had been turned upside down. But she was right. I had totally violated her privacy. And for no good reason, it turned out. "I thought *you* had been in *my* room half a dozen times before. I thought you were stalking me. I had to do what I had to do."

"What? Stalking you?" she asked, breathless. Then she stared at the wall as if she were slowly remembering and processing something. "Omigod, that's why they were asking me all those questions about you and your room and your e-mail." She closed her eyes and shook her head. "They kept showing me this picture of you and Cheyenne with your faces crossed out like the one they found in my room. I was so confused."

"That picture showed up on my desk last week, so when you had one just like it in your room, I thought . . . I thought you were trying to send a message or something."

Ivy glared at me, her black eyes sharp. "I don't know who messed with my photo or yours," she said. "But it wasn't me."

"I get that now," I said, as much as I hated to admit it. I took a deep breath. "Look, I saw the box hidden in your room and I figured you must have gone back to Cheyenne's room to retrieve it. I figured that the broken necklace inside and the box itself could be used as evidence against you, so you stole it back."

Ivy shook her head. "Damn, Reed. Not that it's any of your business, but I got the box in the mail from Cheyenne's mom about two weeks after she died. She knew it was mine and figured I might want it back. I don't even know how the necklace got inside."

I turned and dropped down on the edge of my bed, resting my face in my hands and my elbows on my knees. "I was so sure it was you," I said through my fingers. "I was so sure it was over."

"Well, I'm sorry to disappoint," Ivy said sardonically. "But I'm not a murderer *or* a stalker."

"Then who?" I said, dropping my arms down and looking up at her, my back hunched in exhaustion. "Who the hell killed her? Who's doing all this?"

Ivy gave me a look like it was so completely obvious. "Oh, I don't know . . . Noelle?"

A laugh escaped my throat. "Not this again."

"Why not? She had the motive—wanting to get back into Billings. She knows all the secret ways to get on and off campus. Plus we all know she's evil *and* she has a reason to mess with both of us—me because I turned down her precious invite to Billings, you because you tried to take over while she was gone. Not to mention scoring with Dash," Ivy said matter-of-factly, leaning back against my dresser. "Nice work on that one, by the way. He is *hot*."

"She's not evil, just powerful," I said, ignoring her last comment. "There's a difference."

Ivy rolled her eyes and scoffed. "You really need to open your eyes and see her for what she is, Reed. This whole loyalty thing is pretty pathetic at this point," she said, gesturing at my room to remind me of how I'd gotten there.

"Whether I'm pathetic or not, Noelle has an alibi that's almost as airtight as yours," I said, grabbing my pillows and folding them behind me so I could prop myself up. "She was at a charity event in the city all night, and there are pictures to prove it."

"No way," Ivy said.

"Way," I replied.

"Dammit," she said under her breath. I knew the tone. She was as disappointed that it wasn't Noelle as I was that it wasn't her.

"I can't believe we're having this conversation," I mused.

She looked at me and smirked. "Yeah. Neither can I." She took in a breath and let it out audibly, then stood up straight. "Well, if it wasn't Noelle, and it wasn't *me*," she said facetiously, holding her hands up to her chest, "then who the hell was it? Because if you take the indomitable Ms. Lange out of the equation, you're looking like a pretty good suspect."

I felt as if I had just been slapped and sat up straight. "Excuse me?"

"Hey, if you dish it, be prepared to take it," Ivy said, lifting her palms. "You stood to gain the most from her death. You guys were publicly feuding. You lived right down the freaking hall from her. Who better?"

"It wasn't me," I told her, though I had no real proof. "I mean, I know that sounds lame, but . . . Cheyenne was moving out. She was out of my life. I had no reason to kill her. I—"

"Don't stress. I don't really think it was you," Ivy said, looking me up and down. "You're far too . . . Little Orphan Annie."

Whatever that meant.

"I've looked into a few people, but I'm at a serious disadvantage since I wasn't here last year," Ivy said, strolling the two steps to peer into my broken closet. "I don't really know who she was hanging out with . . . who she was dating. . . ."

"I could fill in some of the blanks there," I offered, without really thinking.

She turned to me, eyebrows raised. "Could you?"

I felt a slight surge of excitement—tentative excitement—and stood. "And you could fill in the blanks from the years before," I said slowly. "Anyone who might be holding a long grudge. People I don't even know about."

For a long moment we eyed each other, neither one of us willing to make the next move. Just looking at her, I was still having trouble wrapping my brain around the fact that she wasn't the enemy. That she hadn't been the one to plant all those awful little gifts and send the e-mails. Ivy Slade was innocent. And, like me, she was also a victim.

"Do you think you could do it?" Ivy asked finally, squaring off with me. "Do you think you could work with your ex's girlfriend?"

Oh, right. There was still the little matter of the fact that she was routinely tonguing the love of my life. It took all my self-control not to cringe.

"If it puts an end to all this crap, then I'll try," I said. "Two heads are better than one, right?"

After the briefest hesitation, Ivy stuck out her slim white hand. "So they say."

We shook on it and part of me felt as if I were making a pact with the devil. But then, the devil would probably have ways of getting things done that I could never even dream of. Maybe a marriage of good and evil was exactly what we needed to figure this thing out. Before our stalker decided it was time to get rid of us—for good.

SENSE

I spent most of breakfast on Saturday morning watching Josh and Ivy and trying to read their body language. Had she told him about our new arrangement? What had he thought of the gift I'd given him? Had he even gotten it? I took small bites of my oatmeal and willed him to look over at me just once, but he never did. He seemed captivated by Ivy.

Which, of course, sucked.

Plus there was no way I could even attempt to get him alone after breakfast, because Ivy and I had agreed to meet back at my room as soon as we were done and try to figure out what our next move would be. I said good-bye to Diana and the others, who were headed to the library to study for finals, and hightailed it back to Pemberly, keeping my head bent against the cold. After making it through the crack security in the lobby, I only had to wait in my room for five minutes before Ivy arrived. She knocked and actually waited for me to open the door. That almost never happened in Billings.

"Hey," she said, shedding her white coat and cabbie hat as she breezed by me into the room.

"Hi."

I waited nervously for her to say something about my gift to Josh. To confront me about making a play for her boyfriend. Just thinking of her being proprietary about him left a sour taste on my tongue.

"I brought my list of suspects," she said, yanking a piece of paper out of her black and white tweed bag. "Of course they've all been crossed off now except you."

She was acting completely normal. So either Josh hadn't received my gift after all, or he'd decided not to tell her about it—which could be interesting. If he was keeping it a secret, that meant it had touched him—that it meant something to him. Trying not to hope, I looked her list over. It was well worn, with notes in the margin and a coffee stain at the top. Clearly she had been working on this as hard as both Marc and I had. Apparently she really did care about Cheyenne.

"I wonder how many other people have taken this up as a hobby," I said, turning and sitting down at my desk.

"What do you mean? Is there someone else?" Ivy asked. She perched on the edge of my bed, tugging down on her short black skirt.

"Marc Alberro. He used to have a thing for Cheyenne. Plus he kind of thinks he's going to be the *New York Times'* next ace reporter," I explained. "So he was investigating too."

"Never heard of him," Ivy said with a shrug.

"I guess that's me filling in the blanks then," I replied.

"I guess so." She leaned back on her hands. "So let's see your list."

I handed mine over. Ivy smirked as she took it in. "So you *did* investigate some of the Billings Girls."

My face turned pink, though I wasn't sure why. I focused on my computer, bringing up a Google search screen in case we needed it. "Of course I did."

"I'm just surprised. I thought you guys were all about sisterhood and loyalty," she said, her words dripping with disdain.

"I'm not an idiot," I told her, snatching the list back from her. "One of my 'sisters' tried to kill me last year, in case you hadn't heard."

"Oh. Right," she said with a trace of chagrin. "Ariana. Who knew she would turn out to be such a psycho?" She looked at me sideways and sat up straight. "Maybe she's the one who's been stalking you. Or us."

My heart skipped a terrified beat. The very idea of Ariana lurking in the shadows of my life made my skin crawl. But I brushed the feeling aside. "Not possible. She's locked up in some asylum or something."

"Or so they say," Ivy said with a leading smile.

I could tell by the twinkle in her eye that she didn't believe that Ariana was really behind this—that she was just joking around. But I didn't like it. The girl had tried to toss me off the roof of Billings last December. That wasn't something I was ready to joke about.

"What if she's on campus somewhere this very second?" Ivy suggested.

With a rush of fresh fear, I recalled those few times early in the semester when I had felt like I was being watched. When I could have sworn I had seen a pair of cold blue eyes staring at me from the stacks in the library, but when I went to investigate, no one was there. Leaving all those things in my room, sending that e-mail . . . those were exactly the kinds of insane things that Ariana might do.

But it wasn't possible. She was safely locked away. Far away.

"Stranger things have happened, right?" Ivy said, loving her spooky conspiracy theory.

"Can I ask you a question?" I blurted.

"Sure."

"Why the hell did you have that picture above your bed?" I said, turning sideways in my chair. "I mean, you hated Noelle and Ariana, looking at Cheyenne's face every day couldn't have been fun, and it was taken on basically the worst day of your life."

Ivy arched one perfect eyebrow. "You have done your homework." She looked down and picked an invisible piece of lint from her skirt, flicking it on the floor. "I kept that picture for two reasons. One, I actually had a good time that day, cleaning up the park. We all did. It's the last good memory I have of Cheyenne, and even of . . . the other two." A blush lit her face for a brief moment and she looked me in the eye. "And two, every time I looked at it, it reminded me that no matter how much *fun* you have with people, they can turn on you in a second."

Her comment hit my heart with the force of a gunshot. She was right, after all. The Billings Girls had turned on me just like that. But then, I had done something awful to one of our own. Ivy had never done anything to hurt anyone.

Unreal. Ivy was actually more innocent than I was.

"Maybe we should get back to what we were doing," I suggested.

"Works for me," Ivy replied, crossing her arms over her chest. "So you looked into some of the Billings Girls, but not all."

"Why would I look into all of them?" I asked, my face screwing up in consternation. "Some of them have no motive whatsoever."

"Oh, I don't know, because they all had the opportunity?" Ivy suggested with a shrug. "Better opportunity than anyone else. I mean, when it comes down to it, the obvious choice is someone who lives in Billings. A random stranger would have a tough time breaking in there in the middle of the night without any of you guys noticing."

"They wouldn't have to break in. It's pretty easy to get a key card for any dorm on campus," I said.

"I know this. All you've gotta do is get into that lockbox in Ms. Lewis's desk," Ivy said. "But—"

"How do you know about that?" I interrupted.

"It was one of our 'tasks' for Billings," Ivy replied, tossing in some air quotes. "We had to make Ketlar keys for all the sisters. It was the easiest thing they had us do. But even if someone had a key, it's not like you guys wouldn't notice that person didn't belong in your dorm. There are only sixteen of you."

I hated to admit it, but the girl had a point.

"I say we check out all the Billings Girls," Ivy added. "Especially considering we have no other suspects at the moment."

Honestly, it seemed like a wise idea, even though I wouldn't be sharing that thought with Ivy. After all, Ariana had been one of my best friends, and I never would have suspected her of Thomas's murder. Never in a million years. So wasn't it just as possible that there was someone else inside Billings who seemed just as innocent, but was capable of horrible things?

"Damn, I wish I still had that disc," I said under my breath, leaning my elbow on the desk.

"What disc?" Ivy asked.

I hesitated for a second but realized there was no point in keeping the disc a secret from her. We were supposed to be partners here. And besides, there was no chance of her ever seeing what had been in those secret files. The disc was long gone. I took a deep breath and turned in my seat, lacing my fingers together between my knees.

"I used to have this disc with all this insider info on all the girls in Billings," I told her. "They gave it to me when I was president. I don't really know why, but . . . Well, anyway, I destroyed it."

"What? Why?" Ivy asked.

"Because I didn't want to have to give it to Noelle, basically," I replied. "It was a whole saving-face thing."

"And you never made a copy?" Ivy said.

"No," I replied, embarrassed once again by my lack of forethought.

"Good thinking, genius girl," she said, getting up.

My face flushed with heat and I actually wanted to pull her hair. Working with her was not going to be easy.

"Did you ever even look at it?"

"Yeah, once. I looked up myself."

"Nice." Ivy rolled her eyes. "On that computer?"

"Only one I got," I said, wondering where this was going.

"Here," she said, gesturing at me to move from my chair. "Let me try something."

She had to be kidding. Like I was going to let her on my computer? Ivy rolled her eyes.

"God, you really are paranoid, aren't you? I'm not going to do any- thing to it," she said condescendingly. "I just want to see something. You can watch every keystroke, I promise."

She was already trying to sit down and if I didn't move, she was going to end up half on my lap. I slid out of there as quickly as I could and stepped back. Ivy opened a couple of windows and double clicked on a file marked "Temporary Files."

"*Et voila!*" she said happily, lifting a hand.

I looked over her shoulder. One of the files near the top was titled "Current Billings Residents."

"No way," I said, leaning over her to click it open. Sure enough, all the files were there, from Noelle on down to me.

"Computers hold whatever files you open for, like, ever as long as you don't delete them," Ivy said, getting up again and pulling the chair out for me. "I'm constantly amazed by how many people don't know that."

I ignored her dig at my lack of computer savvy. My heart was pounding too hard. All this time, all the info I was wishing I still had had been right on my computer. I should have teamed up with Pemberly's resident computer genius sooner.

Not that it ever would have crossed my mind.

"So, where should we start?" Ivy asked, practically salivating to uncover all the sordid details of the Billings Girls' lives. So predictable.

"Let's start with Cheyenne," I suggested, clicking open her file. I had never had the guts to look at it before, feeling as if it was somehow wrong to look into the secrets of the dead. But now I had to believe she would have wanted us to check it out—that she would have wanted us to discover who had murdered her and to make sure that person was punished. "Makes sense, right? Maybe there's something in her file that neither of us knows about."

"Right," Ivy said. But I could tell she was disappointed. Noelle's file was probably calling out to her like the Holy Grail.

Cheyenne's file was longer than any of the others I had looked at. I quickly scrolled through the basic details of her life—her parents' current spouses and former lovers. Their jobs and incomes. Their real estate holdings. Cheyenne's vitals like birth date, hobbies, awards won. The lists were huge. Cheyenne was every bit the overachiever she had always presented herself to be. And then came the list of significant relationships.

"Holy crap," I said as Ivy whistled.

"I knew she was active, but not that active," Ivy said.

The list went on for days. Names and dates. Some of the names had several dates next to them, indicating that Cheyenne had broken up and gotten back together with a guy several times. Many of the dates overlapped. Some of the names were familiar, like Trey Prescott, Ennis Thatcher from Barton, and Daniel Ryan, who'd graduated from Eason a couple years ago. Dominic was on there, as was Gage. There were names of a few other guys from school, and then a ton I didn't recognize. I scrolled through quickly, not knowing what to think. How could a girl my age possibly have gone through so many—

"Stop!" Ivy shouted suddenly.

I jumped out of my skin. "What?"

"Go back," she said.

"God, give me a heart attack."

"Whatever, drama queen," Ivy said, rolling her eyes. "Scroll back up."

Fingers shaking, I did as I was told.

"There." Ivy pointed and squinted as she leaned so close to my shoulder that her long hair brushed my cheek. "Does that say Dustin Carmichael?"

My eyes fell on the name, but it took a second for my brain to catch up. When it did, my breath caught in my throat.

"Dustin Carmichael? As in . . ."

"Amberly's dad," we said in unison.

"Ew!" Ivy proclaimed, stepping back. Her face scrunched up with disgust. "The guy's, like, *forty*!"

I felt bile rise up in my throat and swallowed it back, trying to focus. I stared at the dates next to his name. They covered the two weeks right before school had started. For two weeks, apparently, Cheyenne had somehow conducted a fling with Amberly's father.

"I mean, I know he's like one of the top five wealthiest men in the world, but still," Ivy was saying. "Do you think the two of them—"

"Ivy, shut up a second," I said, my mind racing as I turned sideways in my seat.

"Pardon me?" she replied, annoyed.

"Forget about how gross it is and focus," I said, staring up at her. "Cheyenne had an affair with Amberly's dad. Right before school started. Like, three or four weeks before Cheyenne was killed."

Realization lit Ivy's face. "You don't think that little tartlet could have—"

"Why not? It's a motive," I said, standing up. "Maybe she found out about it and went into a rage. Plus, as we all know, Cheyenne's death left an opening for Noelle to come back, which Amberly definitely wanted. She always made a point of telling everyone that she and Noelle were old friends. Maybe she figured that if Noelle came back and took over Billings, she had a shot at getting in."

"Which is exactly what's happened," Ivy said, her eyes wide.

I felt a jolt of electricity between us. "I knew it! I knew there was something off about that girl. This is why she wanted the disc so badly! She was worried I might find out about her dad and Cheyenne! She was only trying to protect herself."

"Wait. What do you mean she wanted the disc?" Ivy asked.

"I told Noelle I had a copy of this, just to scare her," I said, gesturing at the computer. "Amberly overheard and demanded I give it to her, and when I didn't, she totally trashed my room looking for it."

"Oh my God," Ivy said, paling. "She is a psycho. Although she's not the only person I know who's been breaking into other people's rooms," she added with a knowing glance.

"You're hilarious," I said sarcastically.

Ivy smirked. "But wait," she said, snatching my suspect list off my desk. "You had Amberly on here but crossed her out. Why?"

I blinked at the list. Amberly's name had been hastily added after I noticed her Ariana-esque transformation, then slashed after I had talked to her friends. "Right. Because her roommates gave her an alibi."

"Was it solid?" Ivy asked, gripping the page in both hands.

I tried to recall every detail of my bathroom tête-à-tête with Lara and Kirsten. How Kirsten had thought Amberly had returned to their room at the "ass crack of dawn," and how Lara had quickly corrected her, saying it was still dark out.

"No. That girl Lara was definitely covering something up. Dammit!" I said, my foot stomping of its own accord. "I knew it. I knew I should have pressed her."

I closed my eyes tightly and brought my hand to my head. I had been onto Amberly days ago and I had just let it go based on the crap-ass story of some conniving frosh. She could have easily been lying about the timing of Amberly's return to their room that night. And if she was, it all added up. It all made sense.

"Do you think she's our stalker, too?" Ivy asked.

I had to blink a few times for her to come into focus again. For a moment I had entirely spaced on the stalker aspect of this whole thing. "I don't know."

"Think about it. She kills Cheyenne, then tries to drive you crazy over it, blaming it all on you and leaving all those sadistic little gifties."

I had related all the details of my stalking to Ivy the night before, after we had made our pact. She had been, much to my satisfaction, appropriately appalled by all of it. Apparently the girl had a human side after all.

"Maybe she thought you wouldn't be able to handle it and would move out of Billings," Ivy theorized. "Once Noelle was back, she was trying to create a place for herself in the dorm. Which she also succeeded in doing."

"Plus, by getting rid of me, she could move in as Noelle's new best friend," I said slowly. "And I'm sure her new best friend told her what all the Billings Girls made me do for initiation last year. I can't believe this."

I felt suddenly faint and had to sit down on the edge of my bed. She was right. That crazy beyotch was living in *my* room, sleeping in *my* bed, using *my* private bathroom.

Oh my God. All this time Sabine had been rooming with a psycho.

"But what about the X'd-out photo in your room?" I asked Ivy.

"Obviously she planted it there, trying to pin the whole thing on me," Ivy said, lifting a hand as she paced my tiny room. "Which also worked for a few hours. Damn, this girl is good."

All the pieces of this massively distorted puzzle were finally fitting together.

"I can't believe I didn't see this before," I mused.

"It doesn't matter. What matters is, we see it now," Ivy said. "So what are we going to do about it?"

"We need proof," I said firmly. "Something concrete we can take to Hauer. After what happened yesterday he's never going to believe us on our word alone."

Ivy smirked. "Well, lucky for us the entire dorm will be deserted tonight."

I blinked at her, my skin tingling with realization. "Kiran's pre-party."

"Exactly," Ivy said, sitting on my desk chair and slapping her hands down on her legs. "All we have to do is find a way to get in there and we can check out her room. See what we can find."

"Luckily, I still have some friends on the inside," I said, my pulse racing. I grabbed my iPhone off my desk and speed-dialed Sabine's cell. It went right to voice mail. I wasn't going to get what I wanted from her, but at least I could leave her a message. I waited for the beep and spoke quickly.

"Sabine, it's Reed. This is going to sound insane, but I just wanted to warn you . . . I think Amberly might have been my stalker all along, so just . . . watch your back," I said. "Call me when you get this."

I ended the call and tried Constance next.

"Hey, Reed!" she said brightly, picking up on the first ring. "What's up?"

"Constance, I need your Billings keycard," I said.

"What for?" she asked.

"I have to . . . get back in my old room. I left something in there that I need," I improvised, glancing at Ivy. She nodded her approval at my story.

"Oh, well, I can get it for you," Constance offered.

I squeezed my eyes shut and clenched my free hand. Sometimes Constance's helpful side was really unhelpful. "Actually, it's kind of hidden and it would be too hard to explain where it is. I was thinking I'd just go in there tonight after Amberly and Sabine go out and get it."

There was a short pause before Constance said, "Okay. That's fine."

I looked at Ivy and flashed a quick thumbs-up. "Oh, and Constance, don't tell anyone about this, okay? I'm sure they would all freak out if they knew I was getting back in, even for five minutes."

"I totally understand. My lips are sealed," Constance said. "I'll slip you the card at lunch and just get someone to let me in after."

"Constance, what would I do without you?" I asked.

I could practically feel the heat of her blush through the phone. "Reed! It's no big deal. I'll see you later."

"Later."

I signed off the phone and held it in both hands to stop the nervous quaking. With a grim smile I looked up at Ivy.

"We're in."

REVELATION

Stepping over the threshold of Billings was like walking into my old middle school after I'd graduated. I should have felt at home there, but the sites felt weirdly unfamiliar. Like the place had moved on. Like the very walls knew I should no longer be there. I felt a skitter of apprehension as Ivy grabbed the banister and mounted the stairs. The first step creaked in the silence.

"Reed!" she hissed. "Let's go!"

She was dressed in head-to-toe black like a cat burglar from a cartoon. I was wearing my gold minidress and my long wool coat, fully planning on still making the party bus to Kiran's party when we were done here.

"I'm coming," I replied through my teeth.

Together we raced up the stairs to the top floor, where my old room was located. I pointed out the door to Ivy. My heart pounded like I'd just sucked down eight cups of espresso. This was way too weird. *Way* too weird.

But when Ivy opened the door, it just got weirder.

My side of the room had been completely taken over by the Care Bear brigade. Everything was done in pastels. Pink bedspread, fluffy light blue and yellow pillows, an eyelet bed skirt. Amberly had even had a ribbon tent suspended from the ceiling over her bed, draping down over the mattress like she was some kind of Disney princess. On the walls were framed photos of her and a girl who could only be her little sister, grinning in front of various wonders of the world. The Taj Mahal. The Great Wall of China. The Pyramids. I would have been impressed if the photos weren't so oddly stiff. Like she had Photo-Shopped the two of them into magazine cutouts or something.

"This girl needs professional help," Ivy said, indicating a collection of porcelain dolls set up along the top shelf above my old desk. Their eyes stared out at us blankly from beneath perfectly placed ringlets.

"Let's just get this over with," I said.

"I'm down," Ivy replied.

She turned on Amberly's desk lamp so that we could see without the help of the light from the hallway, and I closed the door quietly behind us. I immediately attacked the desk drawers while Ivy dropped to the floor and pulled a few boxes out from under the bed. All I found was a massive collection of Hello Kitty office supplies. Ivy uncovered a box full of crafting materials and a collection of poetry books.

"Anything?" I asked as Ivy flipped through some of the books, hoping something incriminating might fall out.

"Nothing," she said.

"I got the closet," I told her.

"I'll get the dresser," Ivy offered.

My pulse pounded as I dug through the shoe boxes on the floor and the stacks of books and clothes on the shelves above. Ivy slammed each drawer as she finished with it, and with each slam my heart jumped a bit higher in my throat.

"Would you *stop* doing that?" I whispered.

"There's nothing here!" Ivy replied without apology. Clearly she was already growing frustrated. "Maybe the bathroom."

She turned around and slammed right into the end of Sabine's bed. The mattress lurched and knocked into the bedside table, causing a candle and frame to topple to the floor with the unmistakable sound of cracking glass.

"Shit," Ivy said under her breath.

"I got it," I told her, walking over to pick up Sabine's things.

I placed the candle down and checked the frame over. Sure enough, there was a crack right through the center of the glass. Crap. Looked like I owed Sabine a new frame. I was about to pop it open to remove the shards, when I saw something odd in the photo, right beneath the crack.

I had never really looked at the photo of Sabine and her mother before, except in passing it on my way to the bathroom, but now I saw that there was an extra hand in the picture. A creamy white female's hand. Someone had their arm slung across Sabine's shoulder from the other side.

"That's weird," I said.

"What?"

Ivy came up next to me to check it out.

"Look. She cut someone out of the picture," I said, pointing at the hand.

"Or folded it," Ivy said. She grabbed the frame from me. She started to undo the clasps at the back.

"Ivy! What are you doing?" I hissed, trying to snatch back the frame. "Leave Sabine's stuff alone!"

"We need to throw away the broken glass," Ivy said matter-of-factly.

Ivy finally freed the photo and the glass shards tumbled onto Sabine's perfectly made bed. Sure enough, the photo *was* folded. I snagged what was left of the frame back from Ivy as she opened the picture in front of her. Her face went pale so fast it made my heart drop.

"Oh. My. God."

"What?" I said. "What's wrong?"

She turned the picture around, holding it up in front of her chest. The room around me blurred as I focused in on the photo. Focused in on the smiling face of a pretty blond girl with icy blue eyes.

On the face of Ariana Osgood.

My hands shook as I reached for the photo. Every single inch of me shook. On Ariana's other side was an older man with white hair and blue eyes, who appeared to be laughing as the picture was being shot. Ariana's dad. It had to be. He looked just like her.

I knew what I was seeing, but I couldn't make sense of it. My brain refused to take it in. Mr. Osgood laughing with his arm around Ariana. Ariana smiling with her arm around Sabine. Sabine holding her mother close to her side. They looked like a big, happy family.

"I don't understand," I said, sitting down shakily on the edge of Sabine's bed. My breath started to come fast and shallow, my chest heaving up and down. "I don't understand."

"Did she ever tell you that she knew Ariana?" Ivy asked, sitting down next to me.

"Never. She never said a word," I replied, my mind racing as my skin started to burn. "She's supposed to be my best friend, but all semester she's been keeping this from me. She knows the girl who tried to murder me. She even looks like she's . . . friends with her."

"You don't think that she's . . . I mean, that Sabine is . . ." Ivy trailed off, as if it was impossible for her to say what she was thinking. I was right there with her. It was impossible for me to process it. That Sabine could be our stalker. That sweet, innocuous Sabine could be Cheyenne's murderer.

Suddenly, I found myself on my feet, still clutching the photo. "I have to go," I said, half blind with rage and confusion.

"Go where?" Ivy asked, standing as well.

"All those months I lived with her. All those months I trusted her with everything. And all that time she was lying to my face," I spat. "If she could keep this from me, what else has she been lying about?" I added, holding up the picture.

"Reed, you can't just confront her. We have to call the police,"

Ivy said firmly, stepping in front of me as if to block my route to the door.

"So call the police," I told her. "I'm going."

She reached out and grabbed my wrist. "But the girl could be seriously dangerous."

"I don't care. There are a hundred people at that party," I said. "What's she going to do to me in front of a hundred people?"

"Reed, I can't let you—"

"You can either let go of me, or I can make you," I told her, staring into her coal-black eyes. "Your choice."

Just like that, Ivy released me. And just like that, I was on my way across campus to finally confront the girl who called herself my best friend.

OVER

The music was pounding when we reached the solarium, Ivy trying desperately to explain everything into her cell phone—to make the officer on the other end understand. Red and pink lights flashed, bathing all the faces and distorting them into demonesque masks. Everywhere I looked people were laughing and sipping punch and dancing. Everyone I knew, obliviously prepping for a night of revelry.

But Sabine. Where was Sabine?

"Reed! I'm so glad you're here." Noelle appeared out of nowhere and slipped her warm hand into mine. "I think it's about time we talk."

"No," I heard myself say. "Not now."

A look of consternation crossed Noelle's face, but I didn't have time to explain. I slipped away from her and dove into the crowd. Behind me I could hear her blocking Ivy's entrance, telling her she wasn't invited and she had to go. If only Noelle knew what Ivy had done for me just now. If only she knew how everything had so suddenly and fundamentally changed. But she would find out soon enough.

"Reed! Hey."

It was Josh. Adorable, innocent, kissable Josh in his suit with its open-collared shirt, looking oh so perfectly handsome. He stepped up close to me and lowered his lips toward my ear.

"I got your present. Thank you so much. The paintbrushes . . . the letter . . . it was amazing," he said. "Can we maybe go somewhere and talk?"

I barely even registered the words. Felt nothing at his closeness. I could feel nothing but my rage. And then I saw her. Dancing near the edge of the crowd with Astrid and Constance and Trey and Gage. My friends. She had no right to be anywhere near my friends.

"Later," I told Josh.

I stormed away from him, shoving aside Billings Girls and Ketlar boys as I went. I walked right past Astrid and Constance. Sabine noted my approach, and her entire face lit up.

"Reed! There you are! We were wondering when you—"

Shaking from head to toe, I unfolded the eight-by-ten photo and held it up right in front of her face. Sabine stopped dancing.

"What. The hell. Is this?" I demanded.

Around us, Astrid, Constance, Trey, and Gage slowly stopped moving and looked at one another warily. They couldn't see the photo, but they obviously sensed the tension. Sabine's smile faltered, but only for the briefest of moments.

"Where did you get that?" Sabine asked, her voice barely audible over the music.

"You know where I got it—from the frame next to your bed," I replied, advancing on her slightly, still holding the picture up. "What are you doing with Ariana, Sabine? How the hell do you know her? How could you have kept it from me all this time?"

Sabine glanced around and laughed nervously, as our mutual friends were now gaping at her.

"I don't know what she's talking about," she said, shaking her head.

"The evidence is right here!" I said, thrusting the picture at her. "You can't even try to deny it. Tell me the truth, Sabine. What are you doing with Ariana Osgood?"

Sabine was still smiling, looking at me like I had lost it. My blood was boiling so hot my skin was going to sear right off.

"Reed, I—"

"The girl tried to kill me!" I blurted, my hand quaking. "Tell me how you know the psycho bitch!"

Just like that, something inside Sabine seemed to snap. The innocent, cornered puppy dog mask fell away and was replaced by something dark. Something evil. Something smoldering.

"Don't call her that," she said, her voice hard.

I had to laugh. "Call her what? Psycho bitch? That's exactly what she is."

Sabine got right in my face so fast I almost lost my balance. Her green eyes bored into mine. "She's not a psycho bitch," she hissed through her teeth. "She's my sister."

The world around me was sucked into a vacuum, leaving nothing but me and Sabine behind. The lights, the music, the voices, the laughter, the whirl of color all around me. Gone in a flash. All I could see was the rabid look in Sabine's eyes. So very much like Ariana's ferocity. So very familiar. So very obvious.

Ariana was Sabine's sister. The one she always talked about like she was some kind of goddess, the one she had visited off campus, the one who had been "out of the country" for our fund-raiser. All that time she had been talking about Ariana. Of course the girl was out of the country. She was out of her freaking mind. Suddenly, I remembered a couple of weeks ago when Sabine had tried to get me to confide in her about my breakup with Josh. She had mentioned helping her sister through a bad breakup. Had she been talking about Ariana and Thomas then? My God, I was such a total fool.

"Your *what*?" Constance blurted, bringing me back into the here and now. The world rushed back in on me so fast I thought I was going to faint. And on top of that, the realization. The complete realization of the truth.

"It was you," I said quietly, my hand and the photo finally dropping. Sabine had killed Cheyenne. Sabine had been the one haunting me. She had done it all for Ariana.

"It was all you."

Sabine simply stared at me, but I saw the light of triumph in her eyes. She didn't even seem upset at having been caught. She seemed . . . excited.

"Wait a minute, wait a minute," Trey said, stepping up next to us.

Slowly a crowd was forming around us. Trey. Noelle. Astrid. Gage.
"What do you mean, it was all her? What was all her? Reed, what the
hell is going on?"

I couldn't answer him. All I could do was stare at Sabine. "Why did
you have to kill Cheyenne?" I asked her, my throat suddenly aching.
"If you wanted me, then why didn't you just come after me? Why did
you have to hurt her?"

My voice broke on the word *hurt*, which pissed me off. Trey and
Gage looked at each other, grim understanding creeping into their
eyes.

"Because I wanted you to feel it," she said fiercely, her teeth still
clenched. "I wanted you to feel what it was like to slowly lose your
mind. I wanted to put you through exactly what you put my sister
through. An eye for an eye."

"What?" Trey said. "What the hell are you guys talking about?"

"Let her talk," I said, holding a hand out to Trey. "It feels good to
talk, doesn't it, Sabine? Just like Ariana did. Doesn't it feel good to get
it all off your chest?"

"Don't talk about my sister like you know her!" Sabine snapped,
getting right in my face. "You ruined her!"

There were a few gasps around me as the crowd thickened. Up
until now, it had been difficult for anyone to hear us over the noise,
but now that the other partygoers were starting to take notice, I could
hear the whispers running already, disappearing into the heavy bass
of the music.

"Ariana's sister?"

"Sabine?"

"Reed just said Sabine killed Cheyenne. . . ."

I saw Josh slip into the front row of onlookers, his gorgeous face creased with concern and confusion. I felt stronger just seeing him there.

"Fine. Let's just say I ruined Ariana," I said sarcastically. "What did that have to do with Cheyenne?"

Sabine let out an evil laugh. "Don't pin that on me," she said, shaking her head. "I would never have had to go there if it hadn't been for Josh. All I wanted to do was help Cheyenne steal him from you the way you stole Thomas from Ariana. Easy as pie. But no. Not Josh. He loved you too much. He was too strong. I had to drug him within an inch of his life that night just to get him to hook up with Cheyenne in the Art Cemetery."

All the air rushed right out of my lungs. Astrid's face went ashen and Constance let out a small whimper.

"What? That was you?" Josh demanded, coming forward. "You fed me those pills? You could have killed me!"

Sabine laughed. "Please. You're fine. Get over it already."

I couldn't stop staring at her face, trying to find some semblance of the girl I'd known all year. The girl I had trusted. But there was no trace of sweet, innocent Sabine left. She was all darkness.

"Besides, the pills didn't even do the job! You two still got back together. It made me sick, the way you just forgave him," Sabine said, looking at my feet as if she wanted to spit on them. "That was when I realized I'd have to take a more extreme approach."

"So it's true. You did kill her just to get to me. To make me feel responsible," I said, my palms sweating. A hard rock of guilt settled in over my heart. Once again I was indirectly responsible for murder. First Thomas, now Cheyenne. Both dead because of me. I felt Noelle step up behind me. Getting my back. Just like old times. She put her hand protectively on my shoulder.

"Collateral damage," Sabine said with a sneer. "Necessary in all wars. And let's face it, Cheyenne was kind of a bitch."

Wars? *Wars?* She was clearly out of her mind. Completely and totally gone.

I could barely think. Barely feel. Barely process anything that was going on around me. There was no space. No air. But I needed to know. "And what, your *battle* plan was to haunt me? Make me think Cheyenne was dead because of me?"

Sabine laughed, her eyes wild. "You should have seen yourself. Every time I sent you an e-mail or left you a little 'present.' Things I stole from Cheyenne's room that night her parents so generously let us paw through all her stuff. You were always on the verge of a nervous breakdown."

Someone, somewhere, finally cut the bass-heavy music, and all around were whispers and elbows nudging elbows. I felt tears of anger and embarrassment well up in my eyes. I couldn't take much more of this. All this time I had trusted her. All this time I had thought she was one of my only true friends. But all the while I had been living with the enemy. Sabine had tortured me for months and I had never once suspected her.

My God, she must have gotten such satisfaction out of seeing me slowly losing it. Seeing me lock myself in the bathroom. Watching me tear my dress off before the fund-raiser because the perfume on it was Cheyenne's. She was one of only three people even to know that photo of Cheyenne and me existed, so she must have dug through my stuff until she found it and used it against me. I had treated her like my best friend and all the while, she had been plotting with Ariana.

Ariana. That was how Sabine had known about the blush beads and the bedding, Ariana must have told her. It was all so perfectly, sadistically planned. Sabine probably gave me that stupid rug just so she could crush the blush beads into it later.

Noelle gripped my arm tighter. "You're out of your mind, Sabine."

Sabine just laughed. "Oh, Noelle. Perfect little Noelle. *You* were the hardest to deal with. You kept getting in the way. Protecting Reed. Explaining it all away. Keeping her sane. Acting the part of the good friend."

Everyone was listening now. Everyone silent. I frantically searched the crowd for Ivy. Where was she? Had she called the police? Why weren't they here yet?

"It wasn't acting," Noelle said, her glossy hair falling over her shoulder. "Unlike you, I don't have to *pretend* to be someone's good friend."

"Yeah? So I guess you were a good friend to Ariana, then? When you kidnapped her boyfriend and then became best friends with the slut who stole him away."

Noelle narrowed her eyes. "You have no idea what you're talking about."

"But you know what that feels like now, right? To lose your boyfriend to Reed Brennan." Sabine's eyes flickered between me and Noelle. "Although it looks like you've already forgiven her. I have to say, I expected more backbone from you, Noelle."

My blood boiled. "Shut up, Sabine."

"Reed, you're so pathetically loyal to Noelle I could vomit," Sabine sneered. "Driving a wedge between the two of you was like pulling teeth. But I did it. That video of you from the Legacy was priceless, wasn't it? Girl like you could have a future in porn."

A gasp escaped my lips. One that was echoed by plenty of onlookers.

"That was you?" I said.

"Of course it was me," Sabine said, looking proud of her accomplishment. "I slipped Ecstasy into your drinks and into Dash's all night long. I wrote the note that got you up to the roof in the first place."

Suddenly an image of the note flashed through my mind. The girly handwriting. I had noticed it at the time, but had been too out of it to care. Out of it because of the Ecstasy, it seemed.

"And it all worked like a charm," Sabine continued. "The two of you were so far gone and all over each other you didn't even notice me filming."

The room's strobe lights continued to flash. Sabine's face turned red, then pink, then red, then pink.

"You psychotic, sniveling little bitch," Noelle said from over my shoulder.

"Now, now, just because you totally fell for it, there's no need for name calling." Sabine smirked at Noelle, her eyes wide in faux innocence. "It's amazing how fast you turn on your friends. First Ariana, and then poor little Reed. You ripped her right out of your life without even giving her a chance to explain."

"You're insane, you know that?" I said. "You belong in the same padded cell as your sister."

At that moment we all heard the sirens wailing in the distance. Sabine turned away and my heart flew into my throat. Everyone froze. Everyone but Josh and Trey, who lurched forward, grabbing her to keep her from running. For a split second, I felt nothing but grateful relief, but then I saw the look of terror on their faces. They released Sabine and backed away as she pressed the barrel of a gun directly against Trey's heart.

Everyone around us gasped. There was a scream and a crash as some people raced for the door. I tried to back up but found that I couldn't move. My feet would simply not budge. Suddenly I was freezing cold. So cold I couldn't breathe.

Sabine turned the gun on me.

"Once you were out of Billings, I thought I finally had you. I thought I had finally succeeded in ruining your life. No friends, no boyfriend, no Billings, no future. But you just keep fighting, don't you?" Sabine said, her hand as steady as granite. "After that sappy little speech you made last night, I knew it was time for drastic measures. You're never getting back into Billings, Reed. You can't have the life you stole from Ariana. You just can't."

"Sabine," I heard myself say, breathless. "Don't do this."

"I held this very gun to Cheyenne's head to make her take all those pills," she said evenly. "Now I'll finally have the chance to fire it."

I took a step back. "Sabine—"

"Maybe I am just like my sister, Reed," she said, her eyes filled with unshed tears. "But unlike Ariana, I am going to finish this."

My life flashed before my eyes. Josh, Noelle, Thomas, Constance, Natasha, Kiran, Taylor, Dash, Scott, my parents, my grandparents, even my dog. This was it. This was the end of it all. I would never see any of them again.

"Reed! Oh my God! No!"

The sirens swelled. Josh shoved Gage aside and leapt toward me. Sabine closed her eyes and pulled. The shot went off, as deafening as a blast of thunder.

And then, everything went black.

BEFORE REED BRENNAN CAME TO EASTON ACADEMY . . .

BEFORE THOMAS PEARSON WAS MURDERED . . .

BEFORE NOELLE LANGE RULED BILLINGS HOUSE . . .

BEFORE ARIANA OSGOOD BECAME EASTON'S
MOST NOTORIOUS STUDENT . . .
SHE WAS JUST ANOTHER GIRL AT BOARDING SCHOOL.

DISCOVER THE SECRET THAT CHANGED EVERYTHING IN

THE PRIVATE PREQUEL

Turn the page for a sneak peek of LAST CHRISTMAS,
coming October 2008.

THE GOOD GIRL

Ariana Osgood just wanted to go home.

She knew it was insane. She was, after all, standing at the edge of the ballroom at the Driscoll Hotel, playing witness to the most decadent party of the year. The party she had circled in red on her social calendar three months ago and had been looking forward to every day since. But now that she was at the Winter Ball, watching all of Easton Academy mingle and chat and dance, all she wanted to do was go back to Billings House and be with her friends. Her sisters. Inside Billings it was simple. Inside Billings she could just be.

Ariana reached up and touched her light blond hair, making sure for the fiftieth time that the chignon she'd worked so hard to achieve had held. How could she have forgotten how these events always put her on edge? Always made her feel hot and clenched and breathless. She was going to say something stupid. Or do something wrong. And everyone would see. Everyone would know.

Which was why she had spent the past fifteen minutes leaning against a grooved marble column on the outskirts of the room, just out of view of the table where her friends and boyfriend, Daniel Ryan, were sitting. Sooner or later they were going to notice her marathon bathroom trips and the current column-hugging, and she was going to have to rejoin their reveling. Better make these last few minutes of invisibility count.

Taking a deep breath, Ariana let the sounds of laughter and clinking silverware fade into the recesses of her mind and watched the scene around her unfold like a movie on mute. She committed every detail of the black and white marble room to memory as if her life depended on it. Noting details, cataloging a scene, always made her feel calm, in control.

There were her classmates, stiff and formal in their suits and dresses. The twelve-piece band singing pop versions of Christmas carols on the stage up front. The light December snow falling outside, the large flakes kissing the leaded windowpanes. The waxy mistletoe and the candlelit wreaths that—if she squinted her eyes just so—looked like explosions of gold.

But the curtains . . . well, those she had to remember down to the last filigreed stitch so she could report back to her mother about them. They were exquisite, all burgundy velvet with shimmering gold-thread fleurs-de-lis. Her mother, a New Orleans native, loved fleurs-de-lis. When Ariana was nine, her mother had given her a gorgeous gold fleur-de-lis necklace for Christmas. That had been Ariana's favorite Christmas. The last happy one she could remember. The last one before her father started taking those extended business trips. Before her mother started to fade away. Ariana had never taken the antique necklace off, as if it could somehow tie her to those happier times.

"Whoops, sorry!" A drunk junior in a rumpled Betsey Johnson dress knocked into Ariana on the way to the bathroom, giggling and slurring and groping with her acne-scarred date.

With a blink, Ariana returned to her body, and the sounds of the ballroom rushed her ears at full volume. The band was playing "All I Want for Christmas," and a girl let out a shrill shriek as her boyfriend lifted her off her feet and spun her around. Ariana sighed and pushed away from the cool comfort of the column, giving her teeth a quick flick with her tongue to clear away any wayward lip gloss as she wove her way through the crowd.

As she slowly approached her table, Ariana took a mental picture of her friends. The Billings Girls. She loved to watch them from afar, study their mannerisms, note their tics and gestures and habits. More than anything, she loved when she caught them doing something gross or stupid when they thought no one was watching. Like picking their teeth, or adjusting their boobs in their dresses, or checking out cute-but-dorky Drake boys from across the room. She liked to make mental lists of their imperfections. It made her feel less imperfect herself.

Of course, finding imperfections among the Billings Girls was never easy. It took a practiced eye. They were, after all, Easton royalty. Which meant that Ariana was Easton royalty. She had been ever since September, when she'd taken her place as a junior member of Easton's most elite dorm. Now the Billings Girls, the ones her mother had always talked about as if they were characters in a fairy tale, were her dorm mates. Her friends. Her sisters.

When Ariana was just a few feet away, she noticed that Isabella Bautista, a senior who had taken Ariana under her wing at the beginning of the year, was playing with her violet D&G heels under the table, letting them swing from her toes as she gazed around the ballroom. Suddenly the right one fell off and landed a few inches away from her foot. Ariana watched as Isabelle scooched down in her chair as casually as possible to retrieve it. As she was fishing around with her toes, she brushed Noelle Lange's ankle, and Noelle whacked her boyfriend Dash McCafferty's arm.

"You're playing footsie with me? What are we, twelve?" Noelle joked.

"Wasn't me," Dash replied, flashing a killer smile. "But I'll play any time you want."

Isabella finally shoved her foot into her shoe and sat up again, admitting to nothing, but the snapshot of normality soothed Ariana. She smiled and finally joined them.

"There you are," Noelle said, flipping her thick dark mane of hair over her shoulder as Ariana slipped into her chair. Noelle was, as always, wearing her signature black—a sleek satin Adam & Eve dress that showed off all her curves. "I was beginning to think you'd nicked a bottle of Dash's contraband Cristal and gone streaking through the streets of Easton."

Noelle took a sip of champagne from her crystal flute—the champagne Dash had paid off the waiters to serve their table in lieu of sparkling cider, since alcohol was prohibited at school functions—

and then took a bite of a chocolate-covered strawberry. Noelle was Ariana's best friend at Easton. They balanced each other well. Noelle was more brazen and confident, where Ariana was more reserved and cautious. During their hazing period at Billings, Noelle had helped Ariana through more than one crisis of confidence, while Ariana had helped Noelle refrain from telling off the older sisters on more than one occasion. She was sure that neither of them would have made it through initiation without the other.

"Noelle, streaking is so gauche," Ariana admonished as she took a seat beside Daniel. She smoothed her white, layered Alberta Ferretti dress over her knees and wrapped her hands around the seat of her raw silk–covered chair. "I was just taking it all in. The social committee did an incredible job."

"I swear, if you start rhapsodizing about the engraving on the silverware, I *will* kill you." Noelle groaned and slipped a silver mono-grammed flask from her beaded Marc Jacobs clutch.

"I think it's cute when you go all poetic," Daniel said, draping his arm across the back of Ariana's chair. Ariana looked up at his chiseled profile, his auburn hair, his ridiculously long lashes, and felt for the millionth time the triumph of having a boyfriend like him. They'd been a couple for more than a year, and she still marveled that he had chosen her over all other girls at Easton. "And Noelle . . ." He tipped his champagne flute toward her. "If you kill my girlfriend, you can kiss Dash good-bye."

"It's Christmas. There will be no killing on my watch," Ariana said.

"Buzzkill." Noelle offered the flask to Dash, but he waved it off.

"I have an early day tomorrow," he said, checking his thick silver watch. He ran his hands through his wavy blond hair and blew out a sigh. "I have to be in Boston at six a.m. to meet my father."

"Six a.m.? You are a saint, Dash McCafferty," Paige Ryan said as Noelle handed her the flask instead.

Dash blushed, even with Noelle watching. Paige just had that kind of power over people. Her great-great-grandmother Jessica Billings had founded Billings House more than eighty years ago. Paige, with her auburn curls and glass green eyes, *was* Billings. The true leader. The girl who made even Noelle pause with uncertainty. She was also Daniel's twin sister.

"So what did I miss?" Ariana asked.

"About ten minutes of your boyfriend talking about your Christmas vacation plans. It was lethally boring—even worse than when you get into your Emily Dickinson moods." Noelle rolled her dark eyes. A black-vested waiter silently reached over her shoulder, clearing plates and neatly laying dessert forks over fresh napkins.

Daniel gave Ariana a quick kiss. "Vermont is going to rock," he said with a wink.

Ariana gave Daniel a tight smile, her heart suddenly leaden in her chest. She knew what that wink meant. She and Daniel had long ago decided that they would lose their virginity to each other on their one-year anniversary. But when said anniversary had rolled around back in November, Ariana had chickened out. Of course, she hadn't let Daniel know she was scared. She had simply insisted that she was not about to lose her virginity in a dorm room. Daniel had been disappointed but understanding. The very next day he had invited her to spend the holidays with him and his family at some gorgeous ski lodge in Vermont, promising some serious *alone time.*

Ariana knew what that meant. It meant no more excuses.

The question was, why wasn't she excited about it? After all, Daniel was perfect. He won Firsts every semester, was captain of the lacrosse team, and model-cute, and had already been accepted to Harvard early decision. But the thought of having sex with him made her feel as if she'd swallowed a herd of elephants. That couldn't be normal. Any girl would kill to be in her position, to have a boyfriend like Daniel. What was wrong with her? She studied her napkin—white, silk, Italian—until the feeling passed.

"Well, I'm jealous." Isabella adjusted the strap of her deep purple satin dress. "My parents are ditching me for Turks and Caicos. I'm campus-bound until Christmas."

"You can come to New York with me if you want," Noelle offered with a shrug. "My parents won't even notice you're there."

I wish I could take her up on that, Ariana thought, then immediately felt guilty. She picked one of the decorative red and gold–wrapped boxes off the table and ran the ribbons between her fingernails until they curled.

"Or you could come to Vermont with us," Paige said with a toss of her hair.

She was just passing the flask to Ariana when Thomas Pearson appeared out of nowhere and grabbed it from her fingers. He dropped into the empty chair between Ariana and Paige and took a swig.

"Good stuff," he said, clearing his long brown bangs away from his eyes with a casual flick of his head. "But then, you girls always have the good stuff, don't you?"

"Great. Now I'm going to have to have it sterilized," Noelle groused, leaning over the table to snatch the flask.

Thomas turned and smiled at Ariana, his deep blue eyes merry. Ariana's heart paused. She silently cursed her bad luck. Thomas had always made her uncomfortable. The way he thought he was better than everyone else. The way he constantly teased her. The fact that he was a loser drug-dealer with no respect for anyone around him . . .

"Sterilized, get it?" he said to Ariana, his tone deadpan. He loosened his black tuxedo tie and slung one arm over the back of his chair. "Because I'm ridden with germs. She's hilarious."

Ariana shifted her gaze and inched away from Thomas and closer to Daniel, tucking her shoulder into the crook of his arm.

"Seriously, come to Vermont," Paige said to Isabella, ignoring Thomas as she always did. Even though he was Dash's best friend and came from one of New York's best families, Paige never gave him the time of day. "Save me from being the third wheel to the sappy couple over here," she added, gesturing at Ariana and Daniel with a strawberry.

"Aw, you're just bitter because Brady dumped you the second he got to Yale," Daniel teased his sister.

Paige's eyes flashed angrily. "Excuse me, I did not get dumped. I broke up with him."

Everyone glanced around the table. They all knew that Brady Flynn had booted Paige. Several Yale-bound Easton alums had witnessed the dumping and instantly texted their friends about it. But of course no one would contradict Paige—to her face, anyway.

"So what's the Lange family's Christmas protocol?" Isabella asked Noelle, deftly changing topics before Paige exploded. The last time Paige lost her temper, it had not been pretty. During chores one morning post-breakup she had reduced the normally tough Leanne Shore to tears, demanding she remake Paige's bed ten times until the hospital corners were at perfect ninety-degree angles. Afterward Leanne had spent an hour in the nurse's office with her inhaler, fighting off a panic attack.

Ariana was proud that she had never broken down like that during hazing. Not in public, anyway.

"The ballet, cocktails with my father's miserable excuse for an attorney and his overstuffed wife. The usual," Noelle said. "My parents will probably try to sneak in a little face time with the extracurriculars and write it off as Christmas shopping, meaning they have to buy me more presents. They get a little ass, I get a little Armani. It's a win-win."

Noelle talked about her parents' affairs like she was giving an oral report on the industrial revolution. As if there were nothing in the world that could have been more mundane. Ariana fingered one of her aquamarine drop earrings, envying how everything was so easy, so straightforward for her best friend.

"I can't imagine what that's like, worrying about when your parents

are going to schedule in their 'face time' with their sloppy sides."
Daniel leaned back as the waiter delivered coffee cups and bowls of
sugar to the table. "That's gotta suck."

Ariana inhaled sharply. No one at this table needed a reminder
about how happy and functional the Ryan family unit was. Noelle's
dark eyes smoldered at the dig.

"Well, Daniel, not everyone can have the perfect family, perfect
grades, and the perfect girlfriend," Thomas said wryly, teasing Ariana
with his eyes.

"If we did, what would we tell our therapists about?" Dash joked.

"Or pop Xanax over," Thomas added with a short laugh.

"Like you need an excuse to pop anything," Noelle put in.

Thomas smiled. "Touché, Miss Lange." He snagged a sugar cube
from the bowl and tossed it into his mouth. "What about you, Ariana?
Popped anything lately?"

Prickly heat assaulted Ariana's skin.

"Dude," Daniel admonished, sitting forward to glare at Thomas.

"What?" Thomas feigned innocence with upturned palms.

Ariana forced herself to glance at Thomas. He was looking directly
at her with his searing blue eyes.

Just then a camera flashed, illuminating the beveled edges of her
glass with sparks of light. Ariana flinched.

"Jesus," Noelle snapped, waving her napkin in the direction of the
flash. "Sergei, enough with the stalkerazzi act already. Find new muses."

Sergei Tretyakov stood just two feet from the table, a black Nikon
with a telephoto lens hanging from his neck. Sergei was a Latvian
exchange student and an outsider at Easton. He had dark, sloping

brows, coal-black eyes, and a slightly crooked nose. He could have been quirkily attractive, but he was painfully shy and had a tendency to stare. Plus he always wore these old, dirty tennis shoes no matter what else he had on. He was even wearing them tonight, to a formal event. Ariana could tell a lot about a person from his or her choice of footwear, and Sergei's kicks screamed "street urchin." Still, Ariana felt a certain reluctant affinity for him. She was, after all, a fellow observer.

"Just one more," he said softly in his lilting Eastern European accent.

This time, he pointed the camera directly at Ariana and snapped away. Ariana blushed at being singled out.

Daniel stood up, his chair scraping loudly against the marble floor. "Dude, did you just take a picture of my girlfriend?"

The table went silent and Ariana could feel Noelle's eyes on her. She stopped breathing.

Not again . . . not again . . . not again . . .

Ariana watched Sergei's face go ashen. He backed away slightly, his shoulders curled forward.

"I've taken everyone's picture tonight." Sergei was like a cowering puppy in the face of an irate owner. Ariana couldn't take it. Besides, the last thing she wanted was a scene like the one that had played out in the woods last summer. Not here. Not now.

"Daniel, it's fine. Don't worry about it," she said in a soothing voice.

But Daniel wasn't having it. "No, it's not fine." He fixed his eyes on Sergei and crossed his arms over his chest. "Do you think my girlfriend's pretty?"

Sergei blinked uncertainly. "Well . . . I . . . yes?" It came off like a question.

Daniel's cheek twitched. Several waiters brought out tartlets and crème brulee on silver trays, filling the room with the scent of smoked apples and nutmeg.

"So what do you like best about my girlfriend? Her smile? Her hair?" Daniel's eyes gleamed. "Her cleavage?"

Thomas and Dash hid smirks behind their hands. Noelle and Paige stood up, rolling their eyes at the display of testosterone, and headed toward the bathroom. Isabella whipped out her Sidekick and started texting, probably alerting the other students in the room to the main event unfolding at table one.

"Daniel, stop," Ariana said quietly as Sergei stared at the floor.

"And do you take pictures of all the pretty girls?" Daniel asked, a condescending smile playing on his full lips. "Or is it just my girl-friend?"

"I think I'll go now," Sergei said, backing away from the table.

Ariana flinched as Daniel grabbed Sergei's arm. "Just a second, buddy."

With one quick motion, he lifted Sergei's camera over his head, and started scrolling through the stored images. Sergei made a swipe for the camera, but Daniel held it out of reach.

"Oh, here's a picture of Ariana, and another and another. Isabella—you're in here too. And that's a nice one of Natasha. Hmm. No guys in any of these. Interesting. You know, you're lucky I don't call the cops on you, pervert."

Thomas snickered quietly.

"That's enough," Ariana said firmly, her cheeks flushed and heart racing.

Daniel stared at her for a second, his eyes hard, angry, empty. Then his whole body went slack and he punched Sergei in the shoulder. "Kidding, man. I'm just giving you a hard time."

"So can I have my camera back then?" Sergei looked bewildered.

"A little later," Daniel said with a wink. "I think it's best if I keep it for now."

The band switched to a slow song and the air suddenly smelled like hazelnut coffee. Sergei held out his hand. "You can't just take my camera."

Daniel sat back down and cocked his head to the side. "Dude, you can't just take pictures of my girlfriend."

Sergei looked torn for a second as he stared longingly at his Nikon, then turned away. In his haste to leave he nearly knocked over a waitress refilling water glasses at a nearby table. She glared at him and sopped up the spill with a napkin.

"You shouldn't have done that." Ariana took a sip of champagne, hoping Isabella's message hadn't reached too many people. Hoping they hadn't noticed that her boyfriend had just senselessly humiliated the awkward exchange student.

Daniel held his hands up and laughed. "Hey, I was just messing with the guy. Besides, he shouldn't be taking pictures of you. Not without asking, anyway. Guy has to learn a little respect." His voice turned serious, and he put his hand on her knee. It felt cold and heavy. Possessive. "You know I'd do anything for you, Ari. Anything. Don't forget that."

Ariana smiled tightly. "I won't."

Daniel's words should have sounded sweet and loving. But as Ariana caught a glimpse of Sergei across the room, looking naked and vulnerable without his camera, she couldn't help but hear them as a threat.

WHAT IF ARIANA OSGOOD ESCAPED?

WHAT IF SHE RE-ENTERED THE WORLD WHERE SHE BELONGS?

THE WORLD OF WEALTH, SECRETS, AND

PRIILEGE

WOULD ANYONE BE SAFE?

Turn the page for a sneak peek of PRIVILEGE,
a new series from the author of the bestselling PRIVATE series,
coming December 2008.

NE🛡ER

"It's not fair."

It wasn't a whine or a complaint, just a statement. A statement of the obvious, as far as Ariana Osgood was concerned. As she stared out the window of the Brenda T. Trumbull Correctional Facility for Women, past the maddening check pattern of translucent lines etched into the glass, it was all she could think to say. Outside, the leaves on the trees swayed lazily in the warm summer breeze—a breeze she would be allowed to feel against her skin for exactly fifty-five minutes during midday recess. Recess. That was what the warden called it. Who ever heard of a seventeen-year-old girl looking forward to recess?

"It's just not fair."

Across the wide oak desk, her "therapist" (Ariana added mental air quotes every time she thought of his title) smirked. Shifting in his seat, Dr. Meloni leaned back, forcing his expensive leather chair to let out the loud creak that he *knew* made Ariana's skin crawl. Just outside the fence that encircled the grounds, about a hundred yards from where she now sat, Meloni's precious Doberman Rambo barked nonstop, as always. The inmates of Brenda T. Trumbull listened to that damn dog bark all day long, every day. It was as if Meloni was trying to remind them that he was always there, always watching, even when they weren't in session with him.

"What's not fair?" he asked.

She flicked a glance at "Doctor" Victor Meloni, sitting there in front of his elaborately framed diplomas from schools like Johns Hopkins and Stanford. Her lip curled at the sight of his fake tan. His overly gelled salt-and-pepper hair. His heavily starched blue shirt. His capped teeth.

Two hundred dollars a tooth, but can't spring for a pair of shoes with leather soles. In the sixteen months she had been in residence at Brenda T. Trumbull (nicknamed "the BuTT-hole" by its inmates) just outside Washington, D.C., she had only seen Dr. Meloni wear two different pairs of shoes. The same exact style, one in black, one in brown. Clearly the man thought that everyone he met would be so dazzled by the veneer of his face, they wouldn't take the time to notice his shoes.

But Ariana did. And they screamed white trash turned scholarship student turned poseur. He'd probably taken this job because it meant he'd have the chance to torture the daughters of all the deep-pocketed classmates who had never quite accepted his low-income self at his various fancy schools. And torture them he did. He smiled when they cried. Laughed in the face of their desperation.

Smirked . . . all . . . the . . . time.

"It's not fair me being here for twenty years," Ariana said slowly, stating the obvious. Stating the point she'd made four thousand times before.

"Twenty years to life," he corrected, his blue eyes taunting.

"I don't think about that," Ariana said, averting her gaze again. Outside the window, the lake glinted in the summer sun. A lone sailboat sliced across the frame of the window and disappeared. Ariana almost craned her neck to keep an eye on it for an extra second.

Almost.

"About what?" he asked. "The life part?"

He sat forward now. Interested.

"Yes," Ariana said. "It's unacceptable."

That was when Dr. Meloni laughed. Not just his usual amused chuckle, but a big, hearty belly laugh. Ariana tried not to cringe. She reached up and casually ran both hands through her soft, chin-length blond hair, securing it to the nape of her neck with an alligator barrette. She waited patiently for him to stop, curling her toes inside her state-issue white sneakers. (The most awful shoes in the world—the first thing she would shed when she finally got out of here.) It used to be that she would grab her own arm when she was tense, letting her fingernails cut into the flesh. Then one day last year Dr. Meloni had noticed this habit and pointed it out to her like he was oh so insightful. She hadn't done it since.

"Unacceptable," he repeated.

She looked him in the eye, her gaze unwavering. "Yes."

"You do realize you killed someone," Dr. Meloni said, in the tone kids use on the playground when they challenge other kids to stupid dares.

Ariana blinked, just barely betraying her internal flinch.

Thomas's blood. Thomas's blood. Thomas's blood. Just like that she saw it on her hands. Under her fingernails. In her hair. She had made them chop it all off when she was waiting for trial and hadn't let it grow past her chin since. All that blood . . .

No. She mentally wiped the blood away. Gone. Back to the present.

"Yes. I do realize I killed someone," Ariana said, in a tone *she* reserved for idiots.

What no one here seemed to understand, or cared to hear, was that she hadn't meant to do it. Thomas Pearson had been the love of her life. He had been the only real thing she had ever possessed. It wasn't her fault that Reed Brennan had swooped in out of nowhere and stolen him away. It wasn't her fault that her best friend, Noelle Lange, had come up with the idea to kidnap him and tie him up in the woods to teach him a lesson after he'd humiliated Reed. And it definitely wasn't her fault that when she had gone back to show him how much she loved him, to show him mercy and untie him and set him free, he had chosen to mock her instead of thank her. Chosen to tear her down and act like her devotion to him was worth no more than the mud under his feet. Chosen to push her and push her and push her until she snapped.

If only he'd stopped when she'd asked him to.

"So you took the life of one of your schoolmates, one of your friends, and yet you don't think you deserve to be locked up for life," Dr. Meloni said facetiously.

"It was one mistake," Ariana replied.

"A mistake," he challenged, ducking his chin.

God, she was sick of this. Sick of him. Sick of his tiny little pea-brained, one-sided take on her and every other woman in this hell-hole.

"You see everything in black and white, don't you?" Ariana snapped, her blood rising.

"And what you did was somehow gray?" he retorted.

"I'm not in denial. I know what I did and I'm sorry for it," Ariana said, her words clipped. "But I can't stay here forever. This isn't how it's supposed to be. . . ."

She was supposed to go to Princeton. Supposed to take the train up to Yale to visit Noelle on weekends, or into the city to club-hop with Kiran and Taylor. Supposed to join a secret society. Supposed to hobnob with literary geniuses. Supposed to graduate magna cum laude and snag the job as features editor at *Vanity Fair*. Supposed to live in a loft in Chelsea and meet some gorgeous artsy man who would sweep her off her feet and take her to exotic places like Thailand and India and Sri Lanka. Supposed to be proposed to on a mountaintop as the sun set in the distance. Supposed to have babies and take them home to Georgia to visit her family's estate and sit out on the porch and sip lemonade and watch them play tag under the same peach tree she used to climb when she was little.

This was her life. Her life the way it was supposed to be. It couldn't be over. The very thought made her heart constrict to the point where she actually thought she might stop breathing. Actually thought she might die over the futility of it all.

These were her dreams. Her *mother's* dreams. They couldn't be over. Not because of—

"One mistake," she said again.

Dr. Meloni stared at her. She was gripping the arms of her chair now, her heart pounding. As he stared, Ariana realized that she had just shown emotion for the first time in a year and a half of these daily sessions. She had let the pressure get to her. And Meloni was now smiling.

"One little mistake that *ended* someone else's *life*," he said.

I know. I know this. I see him every night. Every night as I start to fall asleep. Every night I jolt awake in an ice-cold sweat. I haven't really slept in almost two years. Isn't that torture enough?

"I just want to start over," Ariana mumbled, sounding desperate to her own ears. She straightened her posture and stated it more firmly. "I just want to be able to start over."

Dr. Meloni leaned back in his chair and let out an amused yet frustrated-sounding groan. He looked up at the ceiling and shook his head, palms to the sky as his arms lay on his armrests.

"It's always the same with you girls," he said.

"What's that supposed to mean?" Ariana snapped.

She didn't appreciate being likened to anyone else in this loony bin.

He glanced at her, then slowly stood up and slipped his hands into the pockets of his white coat. Watching her the whole time, he walked around his desk and stood directly in front of her. For a long moment, he stared down at her, his expression unreadable. Ariana stared back and felt an unexpected jolt of hope.

Oh, just try something, please. Touch me inappropriately. Try to hurt me. Whatever you're thinking, do it so that I can get your pathetic, low-rent ass fired.

Dr. Meloni leaned down and braced his hands on the arms of her chair. He brought his face within inches of hers. His breath smelled like soy sauce. Ariana wanted to recoil, but she forced herself to stay completely still.

"I have been working with psychopaths like you for the last twenty-five years," he said quietly. "You are not capable of change. If you ever were to be released from this facility, I am categorically certain that you would kill again. So no, Miss Osgood, you are never getting out of here. Not today, not tomorrow, not five years from now. Or ten. Or twenty. Not as long as I'm the one signing your chart. And believe me when I tell you I plan to stay in this job until they wheel my cold, dead corpse out that door."

He pointed at the solid metal door for effect, and Ariana started to tremble. She felt it coming and curled her toes as hard as she could, but it was too late. Tears stung her eyes. She gripped her arm with her nails and gritted her teeth, but still they came. And when one finally spilled over, Dr. Meloni's grin lit his entire face.

"Guard!" he shouted, his eyes still locked on Ariana's.

The door instantly opened, and Miriam, the bulbous Ward Two guard, appeared, filling the doorway. Miriam had an impressive collection of steel-toed boots. Ariana had never even rolled her eyes at the woman.

"You can take this one back to her cell. I'm done with her," Meloni said, disgusted.

"Let's go," Miriam barked.

It took every ounce of Ariana's strength to get out of her chair without collapsing. One word kept echoing in her mind.

Never. Never, never, never . . .

"See you tomorrow, Miss Osgood," Dr. Meloni sang in a teasing voice. "And the day after that . . . and the day after that . . . and the day after that . . ."

He was still chuckling when the door slammed between them.

meet

the ashleys

there's a new name in school

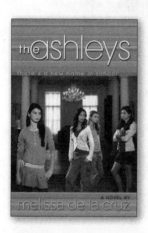

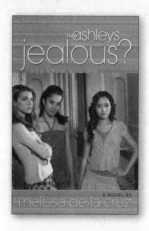

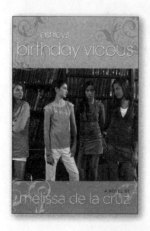

from the bestselling author
melissa de la cruz

He's perfect.

If only he were real.

fake
boyfriend

by Kate Brian

Published by Simon & Schuster